Magnolia Lake

Emily Paige Skeen

Published by Prism Book Group
ISBN-13: 978-1530434596
ISBN-10: 1530434599
First Edition, 2016
Published in the United States of America
Contact info: contact@prismbookgroup.com
http://www.prismbookgroup.com

.

PROLOGUE

In the southern part of Georgia, there's a small town by the name of Davis. This is where I was born and raised, and where I still reside. It's from this town that my friends can't wait to escape. I love this place, though. I love the small, white churches, the historical downtown buildings, and the fact that everybody knows you. I love that there's only one high school and that I've had classes with the same people since I was five. I love sitting under huge oak trees, watching pink flowers bloom on Dogwood trees, and inhaling the sweet scent of honeysuckle. I even love the tiny, run-down corner shops with their chipped paint and worn-out signs.

Not long ago, I would have laughed if someone had told me I'd come to love all these things. Instead of cherishing the quaintness of my hometown, I was dying to leave it. Dreams of a bigger and better life occupied my every thought. I had such different plans for my future, but now I'm happy here, blessed with family and friends. I'm grateful for all I have and simply glad to be alive.

CHAPTER ONE

I screeched to a stop in front of Davis High School, flipped down the sun visor to check my reflection, and jumped out of my baby-blue convertible. It was the first day of my senior year and I was running late—as usual.

A light breeze tousled my long, dark brown hair as I grabbed my purse and school books from the backseat and decided to leave the top down. I hit my car's alarm button and hurried toward the double doors of my alma mater, thinking about how good life was. Not only had I been appointed captain of the cheerleading squad this year, but I was also dating the quarterback of our school's football team, Jeffrey Colton.

Jeff was charming, handsome, and athletic…and the heartthrob of every girl in school. As cliché as that sounded in my mind, it still warranted a smile.

I took a deep breath and pulled open the large wooden doors of Davis High. *This is going to be the best year ever.*

"Cora!" I barely recognized my best friend's voice over the roar of rowdy high school students. I turned around, scanning the windowless hallway for Valerie. Pushing through the crowd, I finally spotted a tall, pretty blonde next to her locker, waving frantically at me.

"Hey, Val!" I exclaimed. "Where's your first period?"

Valerie sighed and rolled her eyes. "I've got P.E. first, and apparently so does Jason Robbins. He caught up to me in the parking lot earlier and showed me his schedule."

Jason had been in love with Valerie since we were all in kindergarten. He wasn't very high on the social ladder, so most girls never gave him a second thought.

I laughed. "Sorry, Val. Looks like you might have to play nice this year."

"Why would I do that? He bugs me!" She sighed and slammed the door of her dull gray locker shut. "I swear he does this every year—I always have at least two classes with him. Tell me that's not planned."

"Well, you know he's just about every teacher's pet." I giggled again. I knew she was annoyed, but the whole thing was hilarious. I could almost guarantee that if she ever gave Jason a chance, she might actually like him. He wasn't that bad looking, just a little on the dorky side.

"I love how funny you think this is," Valerie retorted. "Anyway, what about you? What do you have this period?"

"Calculus...with Jeff." I grinned, thinking about my long-term boyfriend. We'd purposely enrolled in the same classes every semester since we'd started dating in our sophomore year. "I better go. He's probably waitin' for me in front of the gym."

Valerie flung her book bag over one shoulder and tugged down on her denim miniskirt. "Okay. I'll walk with you, since I'm goin' that way." As we walked, we gossiped about which couples hadn't survived the summer, and I regaled her with my and Jeff's plans for the year.

"We should go ahead and get a group together for prom," she suggested. "That way, we won't be scramblin' to fill up the limo like last year. I was thinkin' it should be you, Jeff, me, whoever I decide to go with, Lacy, Mike, Kayla, and Troy. Can you think of anybody else? I think eight's a good number. Four couples. What do ya think?"

I listened as she named our closest friends. Lacy was on the cheerleading squad with Valerie and me, Kayla had been our friend since seventh grade, and Troy was Kayla's steady boyfriend. Mike was Lacy's on-again, off-again fling, but he'd become a good friend of ours during their tumultuous relationship. "That sounds great, Val, but what if Lacy and Mike don't end up goin' together? Which one would we boot?"

She contemplated my question for a minute. Finally, she answered, "Well, Lacy was our friend first, but Mike's so much fun! Maybe we'll just have ten people. They can both bring a date."

"That sounds like a *great* idea," I replied, rolling my eyes. "Talk about drama! No way can that happen. This needs to be the best prom ever. We have to do whatever it takes to avoid potential disasters."

"You're probably right. We'll have to talk to Lacy. Anyway, I better go. See ya at lunch!" Val said. She started into the gym, turning to wave back at me.

"See ya later, Val. Don't be too mean to Jason!" I called after her.

I was still laughing when I heard someone walk up behind me. "Hey, baby, you with anybody?" The low voice in my ear was easily recognizable.

I blushed and turned around. "Hey, Jeff! How was your night?"

He grabbed my waist and crushed my body against his. Then his lips met mine with breath-taking force, only pulling away long enough to answer my question. "It was fine. Doin' much better now that you're in my arms, baby." He kissed me again in a way much too private for the cinder block walls of our small high school.

I caught my breath as I pushed him away and playfully swatted his arm. "Now, Jeff, you know better than that! Principal Long'll be out here in no time, pourin' cold water on us!"

He winked at me and leaned in for one last kiss. He was much gentler this time, brushing his lips softly against mine. "Sorry, babe. You know I can't resist."

Just then someone bumped into him, nearly knocking me down. "What the—"

"Yo, Colton!" Christopher Johnson, one of Jeff's teammates, interrupted me and rammed me against my boyfriend again. "What's up, man?"

"Hey, man!" He turned to Christopher, who was oblivious to my presence. "Whatchya been up to? Where's your first period?"

"I'm headed to English on the 300 hall. How 'bout you?"

"Calculus, dude. Sucks."

I cleared my throat. "Um, Jeff, don't you think we should get to class? Don't wanna be late on the first day," I said impatiently. Out of all Jeff's friends, Christopher bothered me the most. He was cocky and egotistical. He had a habit of sleeping with girls, dumping them, and then bragging about it to all his friends.

"Well, howdy, Miss Stephens." He grinned. "Didn't even see you there."

"'Course you didn't," I mumbled. "Can we go now, please?" I asked, tapping my high-heeled shoe impatiently. The carpeted floor muffled the sound, but the expression on my face was not hard to read.

"Yeah, babe, I'm comin'. Later, Johnson." Jeff turned away from Christopher and grabbed my hand. Once we were out of Christopher's hearing range, Jeff demanded, "What's your problem?"

I came to an abrupt stop and put my free hand on my hip. "Oh, nothin'. Just that every time that guy comes around, you forget I even exist."

"You're gonna have to get over that. Chris is my buddy. We play football together. You oughta start bein' nice to him. Now, let's go." He yanked on my hand and pulled me forward. I didn't like the way he was acting. This was definitely not his most charming moment.

We walked the rest of the way to class in silence. I was pouting and Jeff was being stubborn. We barely said three words to each other during the next few hours, until it was finally time for lunch.

I decided to be the mature one and give in, as usual. "Sweetie, where are we gonna sit this year?" I asked, glancing around the crowded cafeteria.

Jeff's expression was smug. He knew he'd won. "Chris is holdin' a table for us."

I rolled my eyes. Was he seriously suggesting that I sit with Christopher every time I ate lunch for the next nine months?

He made a half-hearted attempt to pacify me. "Don't worry, baby, there's plenty of room for your friends too." He grinned down at me, knowing I wouldn't argue.

Valerie and Kayla were already seated with Christopher and a couple of other jocks by the time Jeff and I got our food. Valerie was chatting it up with Christopher. She thought he was cute, even though I'd repeatedly warned her about his reputation.

"Hey, Cor! Saved ya a seat," she said, grinning ear to ear. I could tell she was stoked that the jerk was noticing her.

"Thanks, Val." I sat down and propped my elbows up on the cold, hard table.

Jeff sat next to me and put his arm around my shoulders. Then he glanced at Kayla, who was being quieter than everyone else. "Hey, Kayla. Where's Troy?"

She looked up from her salad and sighed. "He's got lunch next period. It's the first time in five years we haven't had lunch together."

"Aw, I'm sorry," I answered. I knew Jeff didn't really care about Kayla's feelings. He was only trying to be polite when he'd asked about Troy. "But hey, you've got us, right?" I joked, trying to lighten her mood.

"Yeah." She laughed. "Guess I'm stuck with y'all."

The rest of the day passed just as expected. I had every class with Jeff and a couple with Valerie and Kayla. The three of us talked more about prom, then about homecoming plans. Val and I had one class with Lacy, so we asked about her status with Mike.

"Oh, I'm pretty sure he'll take me to prom," she said. "We spent the whole summer together, and things are gettin' pretty serious. There's no way he'd go with anybody else. Besides, he knows I'll look good in all the pictures, and I've already got my dress." She giggled and flipped her dark red hair in typical Lacy style.

Valerie and I exchanged a glance. We knew how conceited our friend could be, but we usually overlooked it.

When the school day ended, I met Jeff next to my car in the senior parking lot. Pulling away from a deep kiss, I looked up at him and asked, "So what time will you be at my house?"

[10]

"I don't think I'm gonna make it today, baby," he replied, running his hand through my hair and twisting a couple of strands between his fingers. "It's our first practice since camp, so it's probably gonna run long. Then I promised Mom I'd be home to help with laundry."

"Laundry? You?" I joked to hide my disappointment. I'd been excited about getting back into our school-year routine: he had football practice, I had cheerleading practice, and then we ate and did homework together. I couldn't believe he was ditching me already—and for laundry. Something was definitely not right.

"I'm just tryin' to be a good boy, Cora. Don't you want me to grow into a responsible man someday?" he teased.

I batted my eyes up at him. "Of course I do. Because someday, Jeff Colton, you'll be doin' *our* laundry." I reached up to peck his cheek, then opened my car door and slid into the seat. I put the key into the ignition and turned to smile. "Later, sweetie," I said as I pressed the pedal to the floor and sped away.

CHAPTER TWO

The next morning, birds chirped and the sun shone through the window, casting shadows on my pale pink bedroom walls. Despite the beautiful day, I woke disoriented and frustrated. I couldn't remember having any dreams but felt as if I'd tossed and turned all night. I slung both feet off the bed and onto the plush carpet, forcing myself to stand, thinking that I definitely was *not* a morning person.

I slumped down the hallway to the bathroom and turned on the shower. Once clean and presentable, I jogged downstairs and into the kitchen where my parents were having breakfast.

"Mornin', sweetie. How'd you sleep?"

"Fine, Mama," I replied, grabbing a granola bar from the pantry.

"Why don't you sit down and eat with us, Cora?" my dad asked.

"Sorry, Daddy. Runnin' late…I should really go." I held up the granola bar. "This oughta be enough to hold me over 'til lunch. See y'all this afternoon. Cheer starts back up today, so I should be home around five."

My mother gave me a quizzical look and asked, "Will Jeff be here for supper?" She had caught me off guard yesterday when she'd asked why I was setting the dinner table for three instead of four. I'd tried to answer glibly that Jeff wasn't going to make it for dinner, but I could tell she had sensed I was worried. She was all too keen with that mother's instinct thing.

She noticed my hesitation and frowned. "I just assumed, since he didn't come over last night, that he'd be here this afternoon. Is everything all right with y'all?"

"Of course it is," I lied. "Just because he's not here one day... Geez, Mama, you're such a worrier." I tried to laugh, to shake off the strange feeling in the pit of my stomach. "I'm sure he'll be here tonight."

She examined my face and found something that pacified her. Maybe I wasn't as bad a liar as I thought. "Okay, well then...have a good day at school. Love you."

"Okay. Bye, Mama. Bye, Daddy," I mumbled, rushing out the door. My mother was too perceptive. I knew if I hung around much longer I'd end up spilling my guts about the way Jeff had acted yesterday.

The school day began and my worries eventually subsided. Jeff seemed normal again, like himself. We laughed and flirted, held hands walking down the hall, and sat together in his truck after school.

"I've gotta get to practice," I mumbled breathlessly between kisses.

"Just a few more minutes," he whispered in my ear. His hand slipped under the bottom of my shirt and starting inching its way up.

I inhaled and pushed his hand away. "Jeff, stop. Too far. Besides, I really can't be late. This is our first practice of the year."

He sighed and sat back against his seat, staring up at the gray cloth ceiling of the brand new truck. "All right, guess you better go. We can finish this later," he said, glancing down at me. He winked and my heart skipped a beat. Even after all this time, he still got to me. There was something about him besides just his charm and good looks. It was inherent in his personality. He could sweet-talk his way out of any situation, which was probably the reason I always gave in when we argued—and the reason every girl at school wanted to be me.

"Sounds good. So you'll come over?" I bit my bottom lip, that nagging feeling rumbling around in my stomach again.

"You got it. Whatever you want, cupcake," he murmured. For some reason I couldn't quite grasp, the nickname felt more patronizing than sweet.

"Cool, then I'll see you later. Have a good practice. Kick some butt!" I responded—a little too enthusiastically. He kissed my cheek and was out of the truck before I could blink. I sat there for a minute, knowing I should hurry into the gym but too confused to move. I couldn't shake the feeling that something was wrong. Even though things seemed to be back to normal, there was an underlying tension between us.

I sighed and pushed open the door. Straightening my blouse and hair, I grabbed my gym bag and hopped out. A glance at my watch told me I'd have to change into practice clothes in less than five minutes.

Banging the door closed, I took off at a sprint toward the gym. In my haste, I nearly knocked someone down as I shoved the back doors of the school open.

"Hey, kid, watch where you're going!"

I skidded to a stop, looking up to see who had the nerve to call me kid. I grinned when I recognized the face staring down at me. "Hey, Landon! Sorry to bump into you. I'm late for practice."

Landon and I had grown up together since his family moved to Davis when we were in the third grade. We'd actually dated some before Jeff and I got together, but it hadn't hurt our relationship—we were still great friends.

He chuckled. "What's new? I guess some things never change, do they, Cora?"

"Guess not." I smiled. "Good to see ya, Lan. We'll have to catch up soon. I wanna hear all about the girls after you this year."

"Ha. Right. All the girls." He rolled his eyes and put one arm around my waist to give me a quick squeeze. "Later, Cor. Call me sometime soon."

"Sure thing! Bye!" I was already running toward the girls' locker room before the words were out of my mouth. Coach was going to kill me.

Amazingly, I changed clothes and made it just in time to plop down on the hard floor and get into a stretching position before the coach noticed.

Valerie must have seen something in my expression. "Looks like somebody's been up to no good." She winked as we stretched.

My eyes were wide with innocence as I asked, "What do you mean?"

"Oh, come on, Cor! Your face is all flushed," she whispered, "and you were the last one dressed. I may not have a boyfriend right now, but that doesn't mean I forgot how to read the signs. You managed to fit in a quick *make-out* session and still get here with one minute to spare!"

Although her accusations made me blush, the corners of my mouth turned up into a mischievous grin. There was no use trying to lie to her. She had a strange sixth sense about these things.

"Well, maybe a quick one," I answered. "But, in my defense, there are only so many unsupervised hours in a day. Jeff and I don't get much alone time."

Lacy overheard us and chimed in. "Oh, you are *so* lucky! To have such a hot, manly guy. Mike won't even kiss me on the *cheek* at school. He's so worried about what his friends will think. It drives me crazy! I need a little action, ya know. A little adventure."

Coach Rivers shot us a stern glance. Not wanting to be on the wrong side of one of Coach's endless tirades, I focused on the hardwood floor, spread my legs, and continued stretching.

After two hours of running, dancing, and stunting, my friends and I walked lethargically to our cars. When we reached Lacy's car, she hurriedly jumped in with only a quick, "See ya later," before speeding off.

I looked at Valerie, who gave a quick shrug of her shoulders before asking, "So, Cor, wanna ride together tomorrow and go to the mall after practice?"

"Yeah, sounds good. I need new jeans. We can look at prom dresses too! Just for fun," I answered with excitement. "I'll call Kayla and Lacy tonight. Maybe they'll wanna meet us."

We stood in the parking lot, talking about our shopping trip and which stores we wanted to visit. When we finally finished our conversation fifteen minutes later, I decided to put up the top on my car since the sky promised a downpour.

I was proven right just as I exited the student parking lot and the bottom suddenly fell out of the sky, producing sheets of rain that caused me to immediately let my foot off the gas and turn my windshield wipers up as high as possible. It had been perfectly clear for most of the day. Where'd the sun go in such a short amount of time?

As I came to one of the streets I would normally take home, I noticed it was closed due to a wreck. Detour signs were set up a few feet before the crash site, so I turned down an unfamiliar dirt road.

That's when I noticed Jeff's truck parked on the grass to the right of the gravel. My heart started to pound. I knew it was his by the University of Georgia sticker on the back glass. There was no sign of him, but no sign he'd been involved in a crash, either—no other cars, no tree limbs sticking out, nothing. But also no Jeff.

With my stomach in knots, I jerked the steering wheel and rolled to a stop behind the truck. My imagination ran wild as I pictured Jeff being robbed at gunpoint or something else horrific. I just knew he was in a ditch somewhere, left for dead. I practically flew out of my car and around the front of his truck. There was mumbling and gasping coming from the woods several feet away.

I started to panic, my mind racing. A million thoughts ran through my head. Was he hurt? Who was that talking? What happened? Had someone dragged him from the car?

I didn't even notice the wet grass sloshing under my feet and spraying my ankles and calves with mud. It was a good thing I hadn't changed back into my school clothes. I was still wearing shorts and tennis shoes, much better to run in than the high heels I'd sported earlier.

The mumbling noises were getting closer. I saw a path I hadn't noticed before. A car was parked at the end of that path in the woods. I walked closer to the car and peered inside. Through the fog of the windows, there was Jeff. And there was Lacy pressed against him.

My Jeff. My friend Lacy.

I wanted to scream—to yell profanities at them—but my lungs wouldn't cooperate. I just stood there, mouth hanging open, rain drenching my hair, and gaped at them.

"What the—" Jeff pushed Lacy back. He must have noticed me from the corner of his eye. He flung the door open and jumped out. "Cora! What are you doing— Oh, crap! Cora, it's not what you think."

I realized I was shaking my head. Repeatedly. Just shaking my head from side to side.

Jeff lunged for me. He grabbed my shoulders and looked me in the eyes. "Cora, say somethin', baby."

I felt my eyes narrow and my nostrils flare. "I'm not your *baby*." I spat the last word at him and then spun around so fast that the ground swayed beneath my feet. I headed for my car, amazed at my calm demeanor. Although my insides were twisting and turning, I simply walked back toward the road. He tried to catch my hand, but I jerked away. "Don't you *dare* touch me. Ever."

"Just hold on, Cor," he begged. "Let me explain."

"I don't wanna hear it, Jeffrey Colton. Stay away from me." My teeth were clenched, but the words came out clearly. I never stopped walking.

I made it back to my car after what felt like an eternity. He must have stopped following me. I could hear Lacy's high-pitched whining. I assumed she was trying to make him pity her, trying to make him believe this wasn't her fault.

Heck, she was probably trying to make him believe that it was somehow *my* fault. Typical Lacy. I'd witnessed her selfish, harsh actions before. But this time, they were directed at me.

Her earlier words replayed themselves in my mind. *You are so lucky...I need a little action...adventure.* I guess she would do anything to get her adventure, even at my expense.

I didn't know where to go. I drove, but not toward home. When I could no longer control my bottled-up emotions, I pulled over, slumped against the steering wheel, and began to sob.

About ten minutes passed before something rapped against my window. I felt my heart stop as I slowly looked up, hoping to see Jeff even though I wanted so badly to hate him. But it wasn't Jeff. The person peering into my car was Landon. He tapped the window again, so I rolled it down.

"Cora! What's wrong?" he exclaimed, his expression filled with worry and panic. I could imagine what he thought. I was a mess with wet hair and clothes, mud on my legs, and makeup running down my face.

As soon as I heard his voice, the sobs started again. He pulled open my door and knelt down so that his face was inches from mine. "Are you hurt? What happened?"

"Jeff and...Lacy...in the...woods...kissing...I can't...breathe," I tried to explain between hysterics. Landon's expression turned hard in an instant. His head shot up and his eyes scanned the trees and houses beyond us.

"Where are they? That jerk. I'll bury him," he growled.

My sobs let up enough for me to speak normally. "They're not here. They were on some dirt road close to the school."

He relaxed a little. "Oh. All right, let me take you home."

"Thanks, but I'm fine to drive now, I think. I just don't really wanna go home yet. I'll have to explain to my parents..." Tears streaked down my cheeks again.

Landon wiped one away with his fingertip. "Well then, let me take you to my house. My parents are at a dinner party tonight."

Normally I'd argue about inconveniencing him, but I was desperate not to go home. "Okay," I sniffed. "But...where were you goin'? I don't wanna interfere..."

"Cora, you never interfere," he answered softly. "I was just headed to the store, but it can wait. Come on, get in my jeep. I'll bring you back here later."

I took a shaky breath and wiped mascara from under my eyes. "Okay."

He took my hand and pulled me up gently. He stood still for half a second, then his arms were around me. "I'm so sorry this happened."

"It's not your fault, Landon. But thank you. You're such a great friend. There's no tellin' how long I would've sat right here if you hadn't come by."

After a minute, he broke our embrace and helped me into the passenger seat of his jeep. He kissed my forehead and then walked around to the driver's side. We drove most of the way in silence, his hand on top of mine, which was palm down on the seat. Every once in a while, his thumb made circles on my knuckles.

"You hungry?" he asked when we pulled into his driveway.

"Um, sure. I could eat, I guess."

"Okay. I'll make you somethin'," he replied, glancing at me with a soft smile on his lips.

"Landon, you don't have to do that. Really. We can just order a pizza or somethin'." I felt terrible. I hated being pitied, and I hated being any trouble—especially to him.

"No way. You've had a rough day. You deserve a home-cooked meal. How 'bout fried chicken and mashed potatoes? It's the only thing I can really make." He grinned sheepishly.

"That sounds perfect." I smiled in return. We went inside and he started supper while I watched TV. It seemed so natural, so comfortable. He really *was* a great friend, just like I'd told him.

As I thought about our friendship, I realized something seemed different about him. Maybe he was taller or more muscular. He looked older than I remembered. I noticed he was in gym clothes, too. "Hey, what were you doing on that road anyway, Landon?" I called toward the kitchen.

He poked his head around the corner to answer my question. "I was leavin' baseball tryouts. I needed to go pick up a few things, but they had the road blocked because of some wreck."

"Yeah, that's the reason I went that way too." I paused. Baseball? Since when did Landon play baseball? "So you're goin' out for the baseball team? I didn't know you played."

"I've played all my life on rec teams, just never for the school. Figured I'd give it a shot this year, since it'll be my last chance to get a scholarship to play college ball."

"Oh," I replied, surprised. "I can't believe I never knew you played."

He looked at the ground, embarrassed. "That's probably because I quit while we were together. It took up too much time." He hesitated, shifting his gaze back to mine. "Time I wanted to spend with you."

My eyebrows shot up. I couldn't believe it. He had given up baseball—which he obviously enjoyed if he wanted to play in college—to be with me. I'd never even had a clue.

Landon went back to cooking, and I pretended to pay attention to the television. My thoughts were still on this new revelation, so I just stared at the screen, not really seeing what was on it.

Landon interrupted my reverie by announcing that dinner was done. Before we ate, I called home to let Mama know my whereabouts. It took all the strength I could muster to stay calm long enough to get through the short conversation. I knew she'd quiz me as soon as I walked through the door, but I was safe for a while.

During dinner, Landon was good enough to steer the conversation away from topics that would bring up reminders of Jeff. Once the table was cleared and the dishes were put away, Landon and I played board games for a while before driving back to my car. When we arrived at our destination, he cut the engine and came around to open my door like a true southern gentleman.

"Thanks for everything, Landon. And sorry I'm such a wreck. I really don't know what I would've done without you today."

He helped me out and pulled me into a tight bear hug. "Anytime, Cora. You don't deserve what he did to you. I've always known you're too good for that guy."

I nodded slightly, willing myself not to let the waterworks start again. I couldn't handle any more crying in one day. "Thanks," was all I could muster. I gave Landon a quick squeeze then pulled away to get into my car. He held the door and leaned in for a second.

"Cora, I want you to know something. Don't over-analyze this, but..." He hesitated, his eyes boring into mine. "Well, *I* never would've hurt you this way. And I wish I'd had the guts to fight a little harder before you got in so deep with him. I just...wanted you to know."

I blinked. This was unexpected, and I didn't have a response for him. I gazed into his kind eyes and saw all the wonderful times we'd had over the years and wondered why we could never make it work. Maybe there was no spark, no electricity between us. But one thing was certain: there was a bond...a strong, friendly bond. Kindred-spirit stuff.

Again, all I could say was, "Thank you."

Later, I replayed the past few hours for my mom who immediately wanted to call Jeff's mom and "have a talk." I refused to let her, of course. Then I had to go through all the painful details again when Valerie called.

"I *cannot* believe him!" she exclaimed, outraged. "The nerve...what a creep! And *Lacy*! Ugh! I should rip her face off and tear it to shreds. How could she do this to you?" Valerie fell quiet for a split second then sighed. "I'm so sorry, Cor," she said in a softer voice. "I'm sorry you have to go through this. I can't even imagine what you must be feelin'."

I plopped down on my soft bed. "Tons of things, Val. Pain, confusion, betrayal, anger. It was mostly pain this afternoon. But now I think the anger's startin' to kick in. I just wanna hurt him, and burn *her* skin. Burn it so bad that she'd never be pretty again." A small laugh escaped from my throat in spite of myself. I knew my words were ridiculous, and I never would have said them to anybody besides Valerie. It felt good to vent to her. She understood the way my mind worked.

I didn't sleep that night. The image of Jeff and Lacy together took center stage in my dreams.

CHAPTER THREE

The following day was difficult, to say the least. Because the school semester had just begun, I was able to change a few of my classes in order to avoid Jeff. But unfortunately, there were no alternatives for me to take in place of two that we had together—or lunch.

Lunch was the worst. As much as I'd begged the admissions counselor, she insisted all the other lunch periods were full. The only bright side was that I wouldn't be subjected to Jeff and Lacy's "romance," since she had a different lunch period. The issue of table ownership, however, was a different story.

"The nerve!" Valerie exclaimed as we made our way into the cafeteria. "I can't believe he thinks he can stay at our table!"

I glanced at the occupants of "our" table. Jeff, Chris, and two other jocks—whose names I couldn't remember—were on one side. Kayla and Landon saved seats for us on the other. I frowned in confusion. "What's Landon doin' in here this period?"

Valerie chuckled and shook her head. "Boy, you can be really oblivious sometimes, Cora."

"What do you mean?"

"Well, you don't really think he *accidentally* switched to this lunch the day after you and Jeff broke up, do you?"

Rolling my eyes, I contradicted her observation. "Come on, Val. You know it's not like that with us. We've been there, done that. He's just a friend—and a pretty great one, actually," I remarked, watching with a sense of gratitude and affection as he glared darts at my now *ex*-boyfriend.

"Right…a friend. Just don't be surprised if he asks you to prom."

"Shh!" I whispered as we approached the table. The last thing I needed was for Landon to overhear that conversation. He'd probably laugh at me. Or worse, pity me.

Pity—the one thing I'd always avoided like the plague. Hoping to deter that embarrassing sentiment, I decided to take a proactive approach as we came to a halt in front of our seats. With arms crossed and eyebrows raised, I remarked, "Well, I'm surprised to see *you* sittin' here, Jeff."

"Don't be like that, baby," Jeff crooned. "There's no reason we can't be friendly with each other."

My eyes nearly popped out of their sockets at his comment. Furious with his arrogant demeanor, I retorted, "First of all, call me *baby* one more time, and I'll tell your little friends here all about the sappy love notes you used to write me. Second, I can think of a pretty big reason we can't be *friendly* with each other."

He lowered his voice in the manipulative way that always caused me to cave during our arguments. "Cora, you know I care about you. Don't be mad about what happened yesterday. It didn't mean nothin'. Besides, my crew's at this table. Can't we share?"

It took all the strength I could muster to hold back the tears that were threatening to fall down my face. Don't give him the satisfaction, I thought, chastising myself. But it was difficult to keep my emotions in check. I was livid!

Taking a deep, steadying breath, I put my hands on my hips and planted myself as firmly on the floor as possible. "You cheated on me! Why don't we just go ahead and tell everybody the truth?" I accused. Looking around, I raised my voice a notch and announced, "Hey, y'all, Jeffrey Colton cheated on me—with my *friend*, Lacy Garrett!" I was loud enough for at least the table next to us to hear, but I didn't care. I was way past my breaking point. The cafeteria fell silent as people took in the scene. "So, no, Jeff, I will *not* share this table with you. But *my* friends are here, too." I gasped with mock horror. "Oh, *no*...what should we do?" Tilting my head and tapping my chin with a perfectly manicured fingernail, I pretended to ponder our dilemma. "Hmmm...I know! Since *you're* the cheater, how 'bout *you* find somewhere else to eat?"

No one spoke for an eternity, with only the ticking clock to remind us that seconds passed. I stood there, hands on hips, and glared at him. Finally, he gave in.

"Fine, Cora. Have it your way. I don't have to put up with this. Guess you're not over it yet, so I'll leave. Let's go, y'all." He rolled his eyes, grabbed his tray, and stood abruptly.

He and his friends strolled over to a table full of cute sophomore girls who giggled and flirted. Jeff put his arm playfully around one of their shoulders, glancing back at me. My stomach twisted into knots.

"Excuse me a minute," I whispered to my friends. The floor swayed as I ran to the girls' restroom. I shoved the door open and locked myself in a stall.

A few minutes later, there was a knock on the stall door. "Cora? Can I come in?" Valerie asked.

I took a deep breath and attempted to dry my eyes. With shaky hands, I unlatched the lock and cracked open the door. Val leaned in to hug me, saying, "I'd ask how you're holdin' up, but I guess that's a dumb question."

I heaved a shaky sigh. "I can't believe him. I'm not over it yet? How could he even say that? It happened *yesterday*! Ugh! He's such a *jerk*."

"Jerk's an understatement. He's the biggest creep in this school, and probably in the world," Val blurted in agreement.

I smiled a little. I could always count on her to say just what I needed to hear.

"Was that a smile?" she teased. "You ready to take on the cafeteria now?"

"I guess," I answered. "Just let me touch up my face. I can't even imagine what I look like right now."

"Well, you look fine, but sure, make yourself even more beautiful," she replied with a smirk.

"I'll just be a minute. Wait for me?"

"Okay."

I squeezed past her and went to stand in front of the full-length mirror on the back wall of the restroom. I was right about my appearance, mascara ran down my cheeks and white spots marked where tears had washed away my foundation. Sighing, I pulled a makeup bag out of my purse. I contemplated washing my face and starting over, but there were only twenty minutes left of lunch and I was starving. A small touch up would have to do.

Once I'd concealed any signs of a breakdown, Valerie and I headed toward the salad line. Jeff glanced up at me as we passed his newly claimed spot. I met his eyes for a split second, debating. I had a choice. I could be weak and look away, embarrassed, or I could be strong. I decided weak wouldn't do, so I shot him my most devastatingly fake smile.

I heard Valerie let out a soft chuckle. She must have noticed the brief exchange. "Ya know, I'm really proud of you," she remarked.

"Ha. Why?" I asked, rolling my eyes. "I totally lost it earlier. I made a complete idiot out of myself."

She stopped walking and turned to face me, wide-eyed. "What? No way!" she exclaimed. "You stood up for yourself, Cora. That took guts. And you got Jeff to give us the table! Trust me, nobody thinks you're an idiot. I've already heard people talkin' about how stupid he was to mess around on you with Lacy. Everybody thinks *he's* the idiot."

"Really? When'd you hear that? Who said it?"

"I overheard some guys at the table next to us, right after you went to the bathroom."

That made me nervous. It was one thing for people to think I was crazy for making such a scene—that I could deal with. But I did *not* want people to pity me.

I sighed for the hundredth time that day. There was nothing I could do about it. The damage was done. I'd just have to figure out some way to get past this. Some way to keep people from pitying me any more than they already did.

Valerie broke through my thoughts as we filled our plates with not-so-fresh salad. "Cor? You okay?"

"Huh? Oh, yeah. I'm fine." I focused on the food in front of us and tried to relax my face.

"Are you sure? You look kinda strained." She frowned with concern.

"Really, Val, I'm fine. I was just thinkin'."

"Wanna talk about it?" she offered.

"Actually, not right now. Sorry, I don't mean to sound rude or anything. I just can't stand to even *think* about all this anymore. Can we talk about somethin' else?"

"Sure." Silence enveloped us for a minute while we both tried to think of something else—anything else—to discuss that didn't involve Jeff. Prom and homecoming were out of the question as conversation topics, as was cheerleading, since he was the star football player and Lacy was on the squad with us. I cringed at that thought. How was I supposed to go on with normal life? Everything about my "normal" life involved one or both of them. Everywhere I looked, they were there. How could I act peppy at the games while watching him score touchdowns? Especially when Lacy would be standing right behind me, cheering him on.

"Cora. Cora?" Landon had to say my name twice before I heard him. I'd been so wrapped up in my thoughts that I didn't even notice we'd made it back to the table. Valerie was already sitting down, but I just stood frozen in front of my seat. Thoughts—worries—ambushed me. All the things I had yet to realize came crashing down on me at once.

"You all right? Need me to take your tray?" Landon's voice was filled with concern. He glanced at my food, then back at me, obviously confused.

"Oh…no. Sorry. I was just…in a daze. What were you sayin'?" I put my tray on the table and plopped down on the round bench seat.

"I was just askin' what you're doin' Friday night. I'm havin' a pool party. Ya know, one last shindig before my parents close the pool for the season. Thought you might wanna get out and have some fun. Whatchya think?"

"Um, well…Friday, I was gonna—but I guess that won't happen now…" I mumbled. *I won't be going to that outdoor concert with Jeff—not now, not ever.* I shook my head in an attempt to clear all thoughts of Jeff. "Sure, of course I'll come, Landon. Thanks for the invite."

"Anytime," he replied with a smile.

CHAPTER FOUR

The following couple of days passed slowly and painfully. By Friday, I could hardly stand it—the charade of friendly talk, fake smiles, pretending nothing was wrong, when in reality, the world as I knew it was over. Thankfully, Lacy had skipped the remaining cheerleading practices that week, for whatever reason. I couldn't imagine her being ashamed of anything, so it took me by surprise when she didn't show. I secretly hoped she'd quit the squad.

I'd completely forgotten about the pool party at Landon's until school was over on Friday. Valerie and I were walking to our cars when Landon caught up with us. "Hey! Y'all are still comin' tonight, right?" he asked.

"Tonight?" I blinked in confusion. Quickly searching my brain, I tried to remember. "Oh, yeah, of course. Wouldn't miss it." I smiled, attempting to hide the misery already building in my stomach. I was definitely not looking forward to more acting, more fake fun. This would be especially hard because I wouldn't be able to hide behind a lecture or busy work like I could at school. I'd be forced to interact with people, to "have fun."

"Cool. It wouldn't be the same without ya, Cor," he answered, grinning from ear to ear. I couldn't help but return the gesture. I gave him a genuine smile, one of the very few I'd managed since the incident with Jeff.

"We'll see ya there, Landon," I said.

He leaned down and quickly kissed my cheek, causing me to take a surprised step back. He laughed. "See ya, Cor. Later, Val." Then he jogged to his jeep and hopped in. I caught a glimpse of his face as he drove out of the parking lot. He was still smiling.

"Wow, he's real excited about his party tonight," I commented.

Valerie laughed. "Sure, now he is."

"Don't start that again, Val!"

"Okay, okay. I won't say another word. We'll just see..." she trailed off mischievously.

I narrowed my eyes at her. "Do you know somethin' I don't?"

"Nope, just curious to see how things turn out tonight. Ya know, people always couple up at these parties."

"Well, not me. I haven't 'coupled up' with anybody besides Jeff in two years." I sighed. "I'm not quite ready to jump back on that bandwagon." I was grateful when the conversation finally took a different turn as we talked about what to wear that night. Swimsuits and cover-ups, or real clothes and then change into swimsuits? We decided on the second option before going our separate ways.

"Okay, so I'll pick you up at five?" she asked.

"Yeah, sounds good. See ya then."

As I got ready in my bedroom that afternoon, I couldn't stop thinking about Landon. Butterflies did summersaults in my stomach as I considered what Valerie had said. Was Landon expecting something to happen between us at this party? I shook my head. There was no way he would even think that. He was too much of a gentleman to move in on me so quickly after I ended things with Jeff. Besides, no matter what Valerie believed, I knew Landon only thought of me as a friend. He'd said so himself.

I checked my reflection one last time. The bright pink sundress I'd picked out for the occasion emphasized my tanned skin, and I'd spent an hour hot rolling my hair and perfecting my makeup. For some reason, I felt the need to look as polished as possible. I guess I wanted to prove to everybody that I was fine—that I was more than fine—and a good appearance was the start.

"Cora, honey, Valerie's here!" Mama called from the living room.

"Comin', Mama!" I grabbed my bag and skipped down the steps.

"Hey, Val! Ready to go?"

"Ready when you are. Wow, you look great! I feel like a bum." She laughed as her eyes drifted from my dress to her cut-off shorts.

"No way, you look awesome!" I replied truthfully. Her legs looked amazing in the shorts, and the light blue tank top she'd donned worked perfectly with her blonde hair and sea-blue eyes.

"You both look beautiful," Mama interjected. "Now be careful tonight. What time will you be home, Cora?"

"Um, probably about eleven." I shrugged.

"That's fine. Just no later than twelve, okay?"

"Sure, Mama," I replied, leaning in to kiss her cheek. "See ya later."

"Have fun girls!" We were already out the door before she finished the sentence.

"Kayla called and asked for a ride. Troy's got a stomach bug or somethin'. Is it cool if we stop by her place?" Valerie asked as we settled into the car.

"Yeah, definitely. The more, the merrier, especially since it means more moral support." I cringed at the thought of walking into a house full of whispers and pitying eyes.

"Don't worry, Cora. It'll be fine. I'll stick by you the whole night if you want. I won't even get punch without your permission."

I chuckled. "Thanks, Val. You're the best."

"I know. Of course, you may not *want* me to stick around…you know, with Landon bein' there and stuff." She glanced over at me and winked.

"Did you really just *wink* at me?" I asked in mock disbelief. "Listen, not a word about that mess tonight, okay? I don't want Landon to overhear your crazy talk and think I like him or somethin'. I seriously don't need any more drama right now."

"Okay, okay. Not a word," she answered. The grin on her face contradicted her promise.

"I'm serious, Val!"

"All right, I swear." She crossed her heart in a gesture meant to show sincerity.

A quick ten minutes later, we picked up Kayla and then headed to Landon's. It was definitely easier making an entrance with two friends than it would have been walking in alone. It didn't hurt that we were immediately approached by Landon.

"Hey, y'all! Thanks for comin'." He grinned his crooked smile and gave each of us a hug. "Food's that way," he said, pointing toward the kitchen. "But nobody's in the pool yet. Y'all wanna get the fun started?"

"Actually, I'm pretty hungry. Mind if we eat first?" In all honesty, I wasn't ready to change into my swimsuit just yet. I needed to make at least one round through the crowd, or all the time I'd spent on my appearance would be wasted.

"Sure, that's cool. Right this way, ladies." He led us into the kitchen where we each filled a plate with barbeque sandwiches and potato salad.

"This looks great," I remarked.

"Thanks, my mom actually did all of it this afternoon before she and my dad left for their date."

"They have a date?" Kayla asked. "That's so sweet!"

"Yeah. Or gross." He shuddered to emphasize his point, and we all laughed. "Well, guess I'll let you gorgeous women eat in peace. Think I heard somebody jump in the pool. Hurry up or you'll miss all the fun." Landon's voice trailed off as he jogged through the living room and opened the sliding door that led out to the pool deck.

"He's such a cutie!" Kayla commented, turning toward me. "What happened between y'all? You're so perfect for each other, and he's a really decent guy. Why didn't it last?"

"I don't really know." I shrugged. "I guess we just figured out we're better as friends. And then…well, then Jeff asked me out."

Kayla's freckled face crumpled with embarrassment. "Oh, no! I'm so sorry, Cora! I know Jeff's the last person you wanna talk about tonight."

"It's fine, Kay," I said. "He *is* the last person I wanna talk about, but it's okay. I know you didn't mean to bring it up. Don't worry about it." We finished our food and decided to mingle, so we strolled through the kitchen and into the living room. We talked and laughed with some girls from the cheerleading squad, then moved on to chat with Landon's baseball buddies.

Kayla made polite conversation with everyone, but it was obvious she wasn't as comfortable with this specific crowd as Valerie and I. A short time later, though, some of Kayla's friends from the Beta Club arrived and she seemed to loosen up while we talked to them.

We socialized a while longer, enjoying the loud music that pounded in our ears and thudded under our feet. After about an hour, the house became empty. "Guess everybody's outside now," Kayla commented.

"Yeah, so what do ya say, Cor? Should we get in our swimsuits and join the party?" Valerie asked with excitement.

I gave her a wide smile and said, "Sure. Guess I've made good enough use outa this dress for one night." I had actually been having a good time. Jeff had been pushed to the back of my mind, and I was able to focus on my friends. I felt more relaxed and happy than I had all week. It was possibly because I saw only friendly faces or maybe because I felt comfortable—safe—at Landon's house.

We made our way to Landon's bedroom at the back of the house to change our clothes. I retrieved three beach towels from the linen closet—my familiarity with his house was coming in handy— and we headed toward the sounds of splashing.

As we approached the living room exit leading out to the deck, I noticed that Landon's parents had renovated the entire outside area since I'd last seen it. Past the French doors was a large, hourglass-shaped in-ground pool encircled by several lounge chairs of varying hues of blue and green. Tiki torches had been placed strategically at each corner of the deck, and the deck's wooden rails were strung with colorful lights all the way around.

As we stepped outside, I watched Landon throw a girl into the pool. A twinge of jealousy pierced my stomach. Strange, I thought. Why was I jealous of that? I quickly dismissed the feeling, realizing that I probably just felt possessive of him since we were becoming close friends again. I was getting used to being the center of his attention, which I selfishly enjoyed now that I was no longer the center of Jeff's.

Kayla's voice interrupted my thoughts. "Cora, are you okay? I'm sure they're just friends," she said, turning her head full of short, curly brown hair toward the pool.

With falsely innocent eyes, I asked, "Who?"

"You know who," she said. "You don't look too happy about the situation goin' on in the pool right now." As she spoke, Landon and the girl whose name I didn't know—she must not have been a senior—splashed and flirted in front of us.

Val chimed in after she noticed my expression. "Seriously, you're shootin' darts at her through your eyes."

Oh, no, I thought. *Am I really that obvious?*

"Come on, y'all," I answered, trying to play it off. "How many times do I have to say it? Landon and I are *just* friends. We've been friends almost our whole lives. I was just caught off guard…I didn't know he was seein' anybody."

Valerie grinned. "He's not."

I glanced at Kayla, then Val. "What're you talkin' about? How do you know?" My gaze drifted back to the action in the pool. "They look pretty friendly to me."

"Yeah," Kayla added. "How do you know they're not together?"

Val bit her bottom lip nervously. "Um…because I…um, well, I know her," she stammered. Valerie was acting really strange, but I didn't get a chance to quiz her before Landon noticed us and climbed out of the pool.

"Hey! Y'all gettin' in?" he asked.

"Of course!" Val exclaimed. She tossed her towel on a lounge chair nearby and jumped into the water. Watching her with curious eyes, I had a strong feeling she knew something I didn't. I turned to Kayla, who was looking at me, questioning.

"You go ahead," I commented. "I'll get in after a while."

"All right," she answered, inching into the pool one ladder rung at a time. Landon and I were the only ones left on the deck.

"You look great tonight, by the way," he remarked.

I blushed, glancing down at my now bikini-clad body. "Thanks."

"So, ya don't wanna get wet?" he asked, nudging my arm.

"Um, not yet," I said. "I kinda just wanna relax for a minute."

"Cool, let's sit then." He plopped down sideways on the closest lounge chair and patted the spot next to him. I flung my towel where Val and Kayla had put theirs, and went to sit next to Landon.

"So, havin' a good time?" He draped his arm over my shoulder, waiting for an answer.

"Yeah, actually I am." I smiled and poked him. "Thanks to you."

He cocked his head to the side. "What'd I do?"

"Well, you invited me, first of all. Then you made sure I felt welcome and comfortable as soon as I got here. It's been really great to just let go and have fun. You know, forget about everything that's happened. And you made it all possible."

He grinned and ruffled my hair. "No problem. What're friends for, right?"

Every word Valerie had said about Landon still having feelings for me shot straight out the proverbial window at that moment. "Right," I replied, debating for a second whether or not I should ask my next question. Curiosity got the best of me. "So who's the girl you're with? I'm sure she's wonderin' why you're sittin' up here with me." I laughed and tried to sound nonchalant.

He looked confused and glanced around at all his party guests. "Oh." He snorted. "The short brunette?"

I nodded.

"That's my little cousin," he said. "Her family just moved to town. Mom made me invite her so she could make some friends."

It was ridiculous, but I felt relieved. "Your *little* cousin? How old is she?"

"Fourteen goin' on twenty." He chuckled. "She looks older because she wears so much makeup."

I laughed with him. "Well, I know how it is. I remember being that age and wantin' to look grown-up." Our conversation was cut short by the sound of the front door of the house closing.

"I wonder who that is," Landon remarked. "Everybody I invited's already here. Better go see."

"Sure."

He stood and walked across the deck and through the French doors. "Be right back," he called over his shoulder.

Leaning back in my lounge chair, I observed the party. Most people were in the pool, but some had gone inside to dig into the snacks. Everybody seemed so content and happy that I couldn't help but share in their enjoyment. At some point—I wasn't sure exactly when—the sun had gone down. It must have been around nine o'clock. I hadn't realized it was getting that late.

During Georgia summers, even in early September, the days seemed to last forever. That's what I loved about the South: warm summer evenings with a light breeze blowing through my hair, crickets chirping, frogs croaking, and a sky so clear you could see stars for miles and miles. I closed my eyes and breathed in the fresh air. Even though the smell of chlorine was strong where I sat, I could still catch the faint scent of honeysuckle and freshly cut grass. It was the most comfortable I'd felt in days.

Suddenly, the sound of arguing interrupted my moment of peace. Landon's angry words soared through the open patio door. "You got some nerve showin' up here!" All activity in the pool stopped, and people looked around with confused expressions.

"Come on, Landon! Just let me make an appearance."

My stomach twisted into knots and a thousand tiny fists pounded against my chest. I'd recognize that voice anywhere.

"I didn't invite you, Lacy," Landon spat. "You're not welcome in my house after that stunt you pulled with Jeff."

"What?! Why do you care? I thought you'd be happy with me for breaking up the *perfect* couple. Don't you have some obsessive crush on Cora?"

Landon lowered his voice enough that I couldn't hear his response, but I was outraged. Did she really think it would be okay to come to this party? What was her motive? There was no doubt in my mind that she had one.

I hadn't seen her outside of school since her betrayal. She'd avoided me in the halls and had apparently dropped off the cheerleading squad. I decided I needed to give her a piece of my mind, and now was the perfect opportunity. I glanced at Val and Kayla, who were both frozen in place and staring, wide-eyed, at me. As soon as I shifted my weight to stand, they were by my side.

Kayla's eyes scanned my face, searching for a sign of my reaction. "Where're you goin', Cora?"

"What're you gonna do? Are you goin' in there?" Val asked with panic in her voice.

"Well, I can't just sit here, y'all. How would that look? She knows I'm here, and she'll probably figure out that I know *she's* here. I'm not gonna stand by and let Landon take Lacy on by himself. She obviously needs to be put in her place." Even *I* was surprised by how calm I sounded. I spoke as if there was no question of what I should do, as if it was no big deal.

Val nodded then lifted her chin with confidence. "Let's go, then. We've got your back."

"Definitely," Kayla added, even though I could tell by her face that she wasn't as confident as Valerie. Kayla was somewhat soft-spoken and characteristically avoided confrontation.

I nodded in response and we stalked purposefully across the deck, through the patio door, and into the living room. Landon's back was to us, but he turned as we approached. Lacy put one hand on her hip, but I noticed her snobby façade was a little shaken, probably because there were four of us and only one of her.

We stopped just a few feet in front of her, me next to Landon with the girls falling into place on my other side. I linked my arm through his for emotional support, but I was sure she made her own conclusion about the gesture.

"Landon's right, Lacy," I said, my words dripping with disdain. "You *really* shouldn't be here. First of all, you weren't invited." I shook my head. "Now that's just rude, and I know your mama taught you better than that."

"Can it, Cora. I have just as much right to be here as you do." She smirked. "After all, it's a party. More *my* scene than yours."

My anger built up more and more by the second, but I was determined not to let it show. "Bless your heart!" I exclaimed, all sarcasm unleashed. "You really think you have a *right* to be here? Well, nobody wants you here. *Especially* not Landon. And since he's the host and this is *his* house, I think that definitely takes away any 'right' you think you have in this situation."

Lacy blinked. She wasn't accustomed to people standing up to her, and she certainly wasn't used to being kicked out of a party. "And what situation is that? I don't think this little get-together is the real issue here. Why don't you just admit you're mad because Jeff dumped you for me?" She grinned in triumph while I struggled to keep myself from choking her.

Valerie chimed in then. "Shut *up*, Lacy! Seriously, nobody wants to be around you. And for your information, Jeff didn't break up with Cora. She broke up with *him*...after she found you with your tongue in his mouth! Ya know, it takes a pretty bitter person to go after her friend's guy."

Lacy took a step back. She obviously wasn't expecting any lip from Val. Maybe she thought her actions only affected me, that our friends were neutral. "Kayla, do you feel this way too?" she questioned, miffed.

"Of course I do," Kayla replied softly. "What you did was wrong, Lacy. Cora was your friend. How could you hurt her like that?"

Lacy huffed. "Whatever. I'm outa here. This party's lame anyway." She turned to leave, ignoring Kayla's question.

"Lacy, wait." I unlatched my arm from Landon's and took a step closer to her. "I will *never* forgive you, and neither will my friends. After all, they're *my* friends. Not yours. And I don't mean just Valerie and Kayla. I'm talkin' about all the girls on the squad too. I'm their captain, Lacy. They respect me. You, on the other hand, lost any respect they might've had for you the second you stabbed me in the back. So just in case you had *any* intentions of ever rejoinin' us, I'd think twice if I were you." I paused for effect, hatred radiating from my demeanor. "Oh, and have fun with Jeff. I saw him gettin' friendly with some pretty little sophomore yesterday. Don't think he won't do the same thing to you that he did to me. Once a cheater, always a cheater." I turned my back on her to face my loyal companions. Together, the girls and I walked back to the pool while Landon gave Lacy one last warning.

"Don't ever come around here again. And don't even think about messin' with Cora. I suggest you leave now," he said through clenched teeth.

"Fine, I'm leavin'." She stomped toward the front door, slamming it on her way out. A few seconds later, we heard her car crank and tires peel out of the driveway.

Plopping down on the same lounge chair Landon and I had shared earlier, I heaved a sigh of relief filled with emotional exhaustion.

"She has *some* nerve," Val remarked.

I leaned against the cool plastic and rested my head on the back of the bright blue chair. "I know. I'm just glad it's over and I made it through without cryin' or screamin'. Or chokin' her."

"You were awesome!" Kayla laughed. "I had no idea you had it in you. You're always so nice to everybody." She and Val sat down by my feet at the end of the chaise.

I shrugged. "Everybody has a limit, and she hit mine the minute she decided to go after Jeff."

Landon had made it back out to the pool deck and stood by the chaise. "You okay?"

"Yeah, I guess," I answered, looking up into his concerned eyes. "I can't believe she showed up here." Shaking my head, I gave him a timid smile. "But thanks for stickin' up for me, Landon. It was really great what you did."

"It was nothin'," he said. "What else could I have done?"

"Well, you could've let her come out here and ruin my night. Most guys would just let it happen…try not to get involved, ya know."

He stared at me with a tender expression. "Cora, I'm not most guys," he replied in an almost-whisper. In that moment, it was like he and I were the only ones there. Everything else disappeared as I studied him.

I hadn't noticed before, but his body was exquisite. Not buff like Jeff's, but toned and defined. I decided "chiseled" was the appropriate word. I couldn't keep my eyes from his shirtless chest as the moonlight shone on his slightly damp skin. He picked up a lounge chair and moved it so that he could sit next to me. I saw his triceps bulge slightly with the effort.

Kayla broke my train of thought and I was relieved. It frightened me to wonder where that train could have been headed. "Um, I'm thirsty," she mumbled. "Val, come with me to get some tea?"

Out of the corner of my eye, I noticed Valerie glancing back and forth between Landon and me as we sat staring at each other. I gave a slight, indecipherable shake of my head to clear my thoughts, and turned my attention to the girls.

"Yeah, sure. I'm parched," Val responded. With that, they stood and hurried off to the kitchen, whispering and giggling the whole way.

My eyes scanned the area around us. The kids who were still in the pool started getting out, drying off, and heading inside. There was suddenly a light chill in the air, nothing unbearable, but too cold for swimming. Landon stood up, and I assumed he was ready to go inside. I started to stand too, but he put a hand on my shoulder.

"I was wonderin' if we could talk for a minute, Cora," he said.

"Sure." I tried to ignore the butterflies taking over my stomach. I had a strong feeling that I wasn't ready for what he had to say. He moved from his chair to the end of mine and took my hand in his.

I opened my mouth to object, but he spoke first. "Please promise me you won't say anything 'til I'm done." He rubbed his thumb back and forth over my hand, the same way he had the day he'd found me sobbing on the side of the road.

"Landon, I don't think—"

"Just promise," he interrupted.

I closed my eyes and swallowed, leaning my head back on the hard plastic of the chaise again. "Okay. I promise."

I felt his fingers brush softly across my cheekbone and my eyes flew open. He'd said he wanted to talk, but now he just stared into my eyes, inching his face closer and closer to mine. My heart rate accelerated and my pulse quickened as his intentions suddenly hit me with the force of a million bricks. He was going to kiss me. Oh, no, I thought. *Oh, no, no, no, no!*

Then our lips met. My head spun. I had no idea if I'd leaned into the kiss or not. He brushed his lips softly against mine once, then again with a little more force. He lingered the second time and our mouths began moving in perfect rhythm together. They created their own pulse, their own music.

Thoughts screamed in my head. *This can't happen. I have to stop this!* I broke free, pushing him away gently, and gasped.

Landon opened his eyes and leaned back with a dazed expression. "What's wrong?" he asked.

I swallowed and shook my head vigorously. "We can't do this, Landon," I said. "This is *not* good."

His face fell and he let go of my hand. "It wasn't good?" he questioned. "I mean, I know I'm not Jeff, but I thought it was pretty nice. You never used to complain and I—"

"Landon!" I interrupted. "That's not what I meant. We just...we can't do this," I repeated. "You're one of my best friends. I don't wanna mess that up. This would ruin everything. You mean so much to me as a friend, and I wanna keep it that way. You've been great this whole time with all the Jeff drama, and I want you to know I really appreciate it. But you and I both know we're better off leavin' out all the romantic stuff…" I trailed off, waiting for his reaction.

When he didn't respond, I continued rambling. "Besides that, well…what Jeff did really took a toll on me and…I guess I'm still not completely over it. There's a huge hole in my heart that hasn't started healin' yet. I don't wanna use you as a rebound, Landon. You're too special for that. I need to spend this time focusin' on myself, not on gettin' physical with a guy."

Landon looked at the ground, then back up at me, frowning. "Do you think that's what this is about? The physical stuff?"

I shrugged. "Well, isn't it? Hasn't it always been about that? We were great friends who decided to become great friends who occasionally made out. Right?" I asked matter-of-factly.

What I found in his response confused me. His face hardened and his lips pursed into a tight line. "I guess so," he said through gritted teeth, and then he stood and turned away from me.

I jumped to my feet and caught his arm. "Landon, what? I didn't mean anything bad…we both agreed we're better as friends. Don't think that I didn't like being your girlfriend, because I did. I just thought…well, you're the one who first decided we should go back to just bein' friends."

He faced me, sighing. "I can't believe you don't see…after all this time…" he muttered, shaking his head.

I frowned in confusion. He was making no sense tonight. "I don't see what?"

"Nothin', Cora," he spat. "I'm sorry I brought it up. And I'm sorry about the kiss. I should've known better. It was wrong of me to try that so soon after you and Jeff broke up, anyway."

"It's okay. I'm not mad. But what did you mean, I don't see? What don't I see, Landon?"

He inhaled and made an effort to hide his anger. Then he smiled and ruffled my hair to show that the storm clouds had passed. "Don't worry about it. Really, it's nothin'. Guess I was just caught up in the moment, and you look so gorgeous tonight. You're right, though. We were really just good friends that liked to make out sometimes. I was just tryin' to refresh my memory." He laughed. "I'm sorry. Still friends?"

I smiled back at him, glad he was no longer angry but still confused about what had just happened. "Of course, Landon. Forever."

CHAPTER FIVE

I didn't tell anybody about the kiss, not even Valerie. I needed time to sort the whole mess out. I kept remembering Landon's words about me "not seeing" something. And for the life of me, I couldn't figure out what he meant.

I lay in bed the next few nights replaying the scene leading up to the kiss and the conversation after it. I wouldn't let myself think about the actual kiss. I worried that if I concentrated on *that*, I might start feeling things that I knew I shouldn't.

Had I missed something he'd said? Maybe I'd misinterpreted his words or misread his expressions.

Once I finally decided the scene playing out in my mind was exactly the way the incident had happened, I began replaying our romantic relationship from the past. That task was a little more difficult, since it'd been over two years. Nonetheless, I tried to remember every detail, every conversation. I especially wanted to recall our break-up. I thought about that moment several times, but no matter how I tried to imagine it, I always came up with the same end result: Landon telling me that we weren't right together and that there was no spark between us.

I pondered this over and over. Night after night, I tossed and turned, trying my best to grasp the thing I couldn't see. Even after much consideration, I didn't understand what had happened with Landon that night at his pool party.

Over the next few weeks, my life began to take on a new normal. I finally put my confusion and pain to rest and tried to enjoy my senior year. I developed a new routine. Afternoons were spent at cheerleading practice or hanging out with Landon, Valerie, Kayla, Troy, and Mike. When there was no game or other school function, we goofed off at the city park, which was within walking distance from Davis High.

I didn't have much homework since I'd picked a light class load. Although Mama had been unhappy with my decision to take it easy academically, I'd convinced her that I needed a break from the advanced classes I'd taken my whole life. I wanted to have fun and cherish my last year of high school without struggling to keep up with my grades. This year, I hardly needed to crack open a book.

Most of my Saturdays were spent with Landon. We hung out in a shed his parents had built in the woods behind his house. He was working on building a miniature wooden boat for his younger brother's birthday, so I watched him work and acted as his assistant, handing him tools when he asked for them and bugging him with questions. We talked about everything—almost. We never mentioned the pool party kiss or the resulting conversation. I was relieved that we'd finally slipped back into our old friendship routine and that things were the way they once were with us.

The months flew by before I even had a chance to realize it. Christmas and New Year's Eve were difficult since I'd spent the last couple of holiday seasons with Jeff. But with the help of my friends,

I made it through them. I spent Christmas with my family, and Landon threw another party at his house for New Year's. Then in February, Valerie took me out to dinner for Valentine's Day so that I wouldn't be alone. Later that month, I received my acceptance letter to a liberal arts school in New York where I was planning to study fashion design. All in all, things were looking up and my future seemed bright again, despite my heartbreak.

And then it was March.

On the third Friday of the month—a teacher workday, so there was no school—something unexpected happened. I was tanning by the pool in the backyard when I heard the doorbell ring. My parents weren't home, so I was forced to leave my temporary paradise, enter the house through the back, and answer the door. I peeked through the living room window and just about fainted. Standing right outside my house was a tall, gorgeous stranger.

I walked slowly to the door, thinking about how hideous I must look, and stopped. Trying to catch my breath and play it cool, I opened the door to his handsome face. His features were impeccable. He had the most dazzling sea-blue eyes, a jaw line that would intimidate any male model, and a smile that could stop traffic.

"Hey," I said, trying my best to hide the nervous shake in my voice. "Can I help you with somethin'?"

"Hi. My family just moved in across the street, and I thought I should come by and introduce myself. I'm Rex," he replied in a deep voice.

I had to steady myself all over again when I heard him. This guy probably could've said he wanted to rob us and I would've led him straight to the valuables.

"Well, that's very, um…thoughtful of you, Rex," I stammered. "I'm Cora Stephens, and, um, sorry, I'm such a mess…I was just at the pool and wasn't expectin' company." I smiled shyly.

He grinned—I melted all over again—and winked. "Well, I've never seen a prettier mess, if that's what you're calling yourself."

I could feel the blood rush to my cheeks, but he didn't seem to notice. His eyes strayed up and down my bikini-clad body once, quickly, and then landed on my face again.

"I'm so sorry, Rex. How rude of me. Please, come in. Would you like somethin' to drink?" I finally regained my composure, although I felt somewhat exposed wearing only my swimsuit.

He grinned again. "Sure. Thanks."

"Great!" I said a little too enthusiastically. "We've got sweet tea, lemonade, or Coke."

"Tea's perfect."

"Okay," I said as I made my way to the kitchen. "You can have a seat, I'll be right back." As I poured the tea, I snuck a sideways glance at him sitting on the couch. My head was spinning and I noticed my hands shaking. I couldn't believe the kind of effect this guy had on me.

I walked back over to the couch and handed him the tea. Our hands brushed ever so lightly as he took the drink from me, and I noticed my pulse quicken. I thought my heart was going to jump right out of my chest. The immediate spark I felt took me by surprise. I didn't even know this guy!

I bit down on my bottom lip as I looked into his eyes. He was staring at me with wonder. He must have felt it too. "Um, can I get you anything else?" I asked, my voice barely a whisper.

"Thanks, I'm fine," Rex said softly. "Could we just sit and chat for a while? I'd love to get to know you."

I blushed again. "Sure," I said quickly. "Please stay as long as you want."

And he did. We spent the rest of the afternoon talking and laughing. Never before had I felt so drawn to someone in such a short amount of time. I was already imagining what it would feel like to kiss him.

Those were the fastest three hours of my life. When five o'clock rolled around, he mentioned that he needed to get home for supper. My parents would be home soon too, so we stood up to say our goodbyes.

"I had a great time." He hesitated in the doorway, fidgeting with the handle. "If you're free tomorrow, maybe we could do it again?" He seemed nervous. I almost laughed out loud at the thought of *him* being nervous to ask *me* out.

I grinned, trying to hide my excitement. "I'll be here."

"Cool. Same time?" he asked, apparently relieved.

"That'll be perfect. I had a great time too, Rex." I kept my eyes on his, and we stood for a moment, gazing at each other. Then he reached up, paused for a brief second, and brushed a hair away from my face.

"I'll be counting the hours," he said. Then he dropped his hand and headed back across the street.

I stood there in awe and watched him walk away. My heart was racing, and I seemed to be planted in one place. I couldn't get my feet to move and my legs were Jell-O. After what felt like an eternity, I finally closed my eyes, inhaled, and let out a sigh of contentment. When I came out of the trance, Rex was staring at me from across the street, standing in front of his door. He waved, and I waved back, embarrassed that he'd witnessed my awe-struck moment. I quickly turned and went back into the house where I collapsed on the couch.

"Wow," I exhaled. I couldn't believe what had just happened. It was almost the end of the school year, and I'd be leaving for New York in the fall. The last thing I needed was to start a new fling, especially since I'd been burned so badly by Jeff.

I was looking forward to moving on with my life and leaving everything behind. But after one unexpected afternoon, I was rethinking all of that. This person had magically come into my life, and I was already anticipating when I would see him again. I'm in trouble, I thought as I got off the couch to go to my bedroom.

As I climbed the stairs, I thought about his eyes—his blue, intense eyes. Then I thought about his full, inviting lips. Finally, my mind drifted to his toned body. Even through his t-shirt, I could tell he worked out.

I was fixated on Rex when I got to my bedroom, and was horrified when I looked into the mirror to find that I was still wearing nothing more than my bright pink bikini. How had I forgotten to excuse myself and change clothes? Embarrassment washed over me as I thought about how close Rex had sat to me all afternoon. He must have thought I was very indecent, not even putting on a wrap to cover myself. *Great.*

I pulled the strings on my bathing suit top and let it fall to the floor. Then I stepped out of my bottoms and began searching for something to wear. Now that I knew what was right across the street, I needed to look my best at all times…just in case. So I pulled open my dresser drawer and got out my nicest—and shortest—pair of shorts. They were a light blue dressy material. I put on a white tank top rimmed with lace and stared at myself in the mirror. Not too bad, I thought. Tanning in the sun the past couple of afternoons had paid off. The pale colors of the clothes complimented my skin. I'd always been amazed at how different having even a little bit of color could make my appearance. It gave me a sense of confidence that I didn't otherwise possess.

I smiled at my reflection, secretly hoping *he* would just happen to spend the evening outside. I slipped on a pair of white wedge sandals and headed back downstairs, just in time to hear my mother's car pull in the driveway. She'd been out shopping with my aunt all afternoon. I knew my father would be home soon because Mama always gave herself enough time to have supper ready, or at least started, when Daddy walked through the door each night. I respected her loyalty and diligence as a housewife, but thought I'd never be able to live that way.

"Cora?" Mama called out as she opened the front door.

"I'm comin'." I jogged the rest of the way down the steps and met her in the living room. "Hey, Mama," I said as she leaned in to kiss my cheek.

"Well, don't you look spiffy," she exclaimed with a surprised look. "Do you have plans tonight?"

"Um, nope, no plans. Just felt like lookin' nice today." I knew it was pointless to lie. She would see right through me.

"Mm-hmm." She grinned. "This wouldn't have anything to do with that new family that just moved in across the street, would it? I hear they have a son about your age."

"Mama," I exclaimed, "don't be silly! Why would I get all dressed up for some boy I don't even know?"

My mother just stared at me with that knowing look she always got when she could tell I wasn't giving her the whole story.

"Okay, okay." I sighed. "His name's Rex. He stopped by this afternoon to introduce himself. I invited him in for somethin' to drink and we talked for a few hours."

"A few hours?" Mama laughed.

"Yeah," I replied, remembering the afternoon. "We just sat on the couch and talked and talked. Before I knew it, it was almost five o'clock. Mama, he's so amazin'. Gorgeous, funny, polite…." I didn't mention how inviting I found his lips.

"Now, Cora. Don't go gettin' yourself wrapped up in some boy. I know a summer romance might seem like fun right now, but I don't want you gettin' your heart broken just a few months before you leave for college. I especially don't want you goin' through another situation like the one with Jeff."

"Oh, Mama. I'm not sayin' I wanna marry the guy. All I'm sayin' is he's really cute and nice. You don't need to worry."

"Just promise me you won't get in too deep, Cora," she said with a stern look. "Besides, you've been spendin' an awful lot of time with Landon lately. You need to be careful not to spread yourself too thin. And remember, it's my job to worry. So do me a favor and guard your heart. Promise me, Cora."

"Promise." Too late, I thought, even as I said the word. I was already in too deep and I'd only spent one day with Rex. "So what's for supper?" I asked to change the subject.

"Well, your daddy wants lasagna. Is that okay with you?"

"Sure, whatever y'all want is fine." I smiled with relief that the subject of Rex was closed, but suddenly, there was a cloud over my sunny mood. The mention of Landon gave me a nagging feeling that I couldn't quite understand.

Just then, my father walked through the front door. "There's my two favorite girls!" he exclaimed with a grin. He leaned in to kiss Mama and then hugged my neck.

"Hey, Daddy. How was work?" I asked, hoping my mother wouldn't mention anything about our new neighbors.

"It was fine. Won my case today."

"The one you've been workin' on for so long? That's great!" Daddy was an attorney at the most prominent law firm in Davis.

"Yep, that's the one. So what are you all fancied up for?"

Oh, great, here we go again. "Geez, can't a girl look nice sometimes without gettin' interrogated?" I laughed, hoping he would let it go.

"Sure she can, and a father can interrogate," he answered with a chuckle.

"She's goin' to Valerie's," Mama said. I glanced at her with raised eyebrows, shocked at the lie.

"Yep, goin' to Val's," I chimed in. "We were thinking about seein' a movie." I couldn't believe my conservative, no-nonsense mother was scheming for me.

"Okay, well don't be out past midnight. And be careful. All kinds a' things can happen to two young girls goin' out at night alone," Daddy replied.

"You worry too much. We'll be fine," I said, relieved that Rex wouldn't be mentioned again. My father sighed and shook his head, mumbling something about dangerous people as he walked out of the room. I looked at Mama. "What was that all about? I haven't even talked to Val today."

"We're not gonna bother your daddy about some boy you just think is 'cute and nice.' You know how he is. He'll constantly worry about leavin' you alone with that Rex right across the street."

"Oh. Well, thanks, Mama." I was surprised that she would hide anything from my father. They were always so open with each other. Normally, I couldn't tell her anything I didn't want him to know. I hugged her. "Well, I guess I'll go call Valerie and see if she wants to go out."

Mama laughed. "That's probably a good idea."

I headed to my bedroom where I could make the call in private. After closing the door securely, I picked up my cell phone. Because I knew Valerie well, I assumed she wouldn't have her cell nearby — she was constantly losing it. So to be on the safe side, I dialed her home number. It rang twice before Val's mom picked up. "Hey, Ms. Laura," I greeted her. "This is Cora."

"Oh, Cora! How are you, honey?" she crooned. Laura was a stay-at-home mom, like mine. They were both true southern women. They baked, cleaned…the whole nine yards. They'd been friends since before Valerie and I were born. And Laura always called people "honey."

"I'm fine. Is Val there?"

"Sure, hang on just a sec," she answered before I heard her call for Valerie.

"Hey, Cora. What's up?" Valerie's voice sounded strange, almost nervous.

"Well, it's kind of a long story, but you and I need to go see a movie tonight."

"Oh, a movie. That's great! I was afraid… Anyway, why do we *need* to see a movie?" She laughed.

"Well, that's what Mama told Daddy I was doin', so that he wouldn't know about the hot guy I met today." I knew my friend well. As soon as I mentioned a guy she was all ears.

"What hot guy? Cora, explain now!" she demanded.

"I'll tell you everything, but you have to go to the movies with me, or at least get me out of the house. And then I'll give you all the juicy details." I laughed.

"It's a deal!" she exclaimed. "Do you want me to pick you up or meet there?"

"I'll drive over to your house so we can ride together. I need to get away from here now before I get another lecture from my mother about the importance of guardin' my heart."

"Okay, see ya in a few!"

"I'll be there in ten minutes." I hung up the phone and grabbed my purse. Stopping in front of the mirror, I decided to put on a little more makeup, just in case Rex was outside. I finished primping and ran down the stairs. "I'm gone!" I called out.

"Okay, have fun, Cora," Mama replied. "Wait, here's thirty dollars. Pay for Valerie's ticket too."

"Thanks, Mama. Love you." I was out the door in a hurry. I jumped in my car and cranked her up. Just as I started to back out, I caught a glimpse of Rex in the rearview mirror. He was pushing a young girl, whom I assumed was his little sister, on their swing. I waved as I turned onto the street and he watched me drive away.

A short ten minutes later, I pulled onto Valerie's driveway. She was already waiting for me on the front porch. "Let's go." She hurried me back toward the car before I even made it to the porch steps.

"Oh, I was gonna go say hey to your mom," I said, wondering what the rush was.

"No, forget about that. I wanna hear all about this guy. Besides, Mama's doin' her yoga."

I laughed. "Okay, then, I guess we'll go." We jumped in my car and I threw it in reverse. "Girl's night!"

CHAPTER SIX

"So...start from the beginning." Valerie was being extra pushy about this Rex thing. I had no idea why, but she seemed even more interested in the situation than she would be normally.

"Okay, but first tell me why in the world you're bein' so bossy," I joked. "There's no rush, we have all night."

"Cor." She sighed. "I didn't want to tell you this. In fact, I've been debatin' over it all day." She was suddenly completely serious.

The expression on her face was making me nervous, and I had a sick feeling in the pit of my stomach. "What is it? Is somethin' wrong?"

"I don't know." She shrugged. "Maybe it's not a good idea to tell you now. Maybe I should wait until after the movie. So tell me about this handsome man you met today! Where did you meet him? What does he look like? How old is he? What color—"

"Val!" I interrupted. "You're kinda freakin' me out. *What* is goin' on? Tell me now or I'll pull this car over right here!" I almost laughed out loud when I realized how much I sounded like my mother in that instant.

I *almost* laughed out loud, but something in Val's eyes made me stop short.

She hesitated. It felt like an eternity before she said anything else. I sensed she was debating, weighing the pros and cons, so I gave her a minute. We were only a mile away from the movie theater when she finally spoke.

"Cora, Lacy called me this morning."

I gasped, whipped my head around to gawk at her, and involuntarily slammed on the brakes. It was a good thing no one was behind us. I quickly regained my composure, glanced in the rearview mirror, and pulled to the side of the road.

"What did she say?" I asked slowly.

Valerie sighed. Her pained expression made me nauseous. "She...said...Jeff proposed to her."

I couldn't breathe. I couldn't think. I definitely couldn't drive. I just sat, staring at the road in front of us. I don't know how long we stayed that way.

A million emotions raced through me. The first was rage. How *dare* he do this to me! Why her? He knew she used to be my friend. And Lacy! What a friend she turned out to be! Why would she even tell Valerie, when she knew Valerie would never keep a secret from me?

Then the disbelief set in. They were only eighteen! There was no way his parents would approve of him getting married. We hadn't even graduated high school yet.

The last—but strongest—emotion I felt was pain. Horrific, physically disabling pain. My breathing became heavy and I felt as if I would vomit. I closed my eyes and took a deep breath, which came out in a rush.

"Cor?" Valerie was eyeing me carefully, not sure what to do. "Are you okay? You look like...you look sick."

"I *am* sick, Val," I managed to whisper. "He was supposed to marry *me*." And then the sobbing started. "We were supposed to graduate, go to college together, and get married! Now he's gonna marry *her*. And they're only eighteen! I can't believe this is happening." The sobbing was completely out of control by this point. I was having trouble catching my breath.

"Shhh, it's okay." Valerie put her arms around me and patted my hair, trying to comfort me. "You're so much better than him, Cora. You deserve someone who'll cherish you. Ya know, worship the ground you walk on. He's nothin' but scum. It's a good thing this happened now if you think about it. I mean, what if y'all had gone through a year of college together, and then he did somethin' idiotic like this? You'd be stuck in the same town with him for the rest of your college career. At least now you can get away from him. Get him—and her—out of your head once and for all."

I leaned away from Valerie, opening my eyes slowly. I tried to steady my breathing and get myself back under control. "You're right," I said. "This is ridiculous. I've already wasted too much time and too many tears on him. Let's go see that movie."

"Are you sure you're all right?" Valerie asked. "We don't have to do this. We can go back to my house if you want." Valerie looked worried, as if she thought I would break down again any second. "I've got ice cream."

"No, Val, I'm fine." *Or at least I'll pretend to be.* "Besides, a movie's the perfect way to get my mind off this. I need to escape my thoughts for a while." I put the car in drive and inched back onto the road.

"Okay, if that's what you wanna do." Valerie still looked doubtful, but I drove to the theater anyway. I had to do *something*. I couldn't sit around and talk about it or even think about it.

The movie didn't help much. We'd picked a romantic comedy, because I had been in the mood for romance after I met Rex. But as it was, I sunk into a deep depression during the movie. I kept thinking about the sweet things Jeff used to do for me and how perfect our relationship had been before Lacy wrecked it. By the time the lights came on, I was past depression. I was numb. I felt like a zombie walking back to the car outside the theater. Valerie asked if she should drive and I said yes.

"I'm sorry about that movie," she commented after starting the car.

"What do you mean?" I asked innocently.

"Come on, Cor. You looked green durin' the whole thing. At one point, I thought you were gonna double over in pain, your face was so tense."

"Oh. Sorry about that. I'm fine now. Sorry."

"What? You don't have to apologize, Cora. I'm not angry. I mean, nobody would expect you to sit through that movie and be 'fine' after what you just found out."

"Thanks, Val." I sighed. "I don't mean to sound rude, but can we drop it now? I don't think I can stand to talk about it anymore tonight."

"Sure, of course." She paused, and then looked at me with a grin. "So tell me about this gorgeous new man of yours."

I smiled a little, in spite of myself. "Well, he's not *my* man. But he *is* gorgeous." I continued the story, telling Valerie exactly what had taken place that afternoon and not leaving out a single detail. I discovered, amazingly, that talking about him made me feel better. While my mind was focused on Rex, I didn't even care that Jeff was getting married. Amazing.

"Whoa," Valerie said when I finished the story. "Sounds like you've got it bad."

"Yeah," I mumbled with a sigh. "I'm afraid so."

CHAPTER SEVEN

The following morning, I awoke with tear streaks down my face and mascara stains on my pillow. I'd spent the whole night in and out of dreams. Nightmares, actually. At one point, my subconscious placed me in an empty church, dressed in a wedding gown, and waiting for Jeff to arrive. He never did.

In another dream, I went to Jeff's house and found him laughing and playing with some kids. I walked into the house to greet my children and husband, and then Lacy was there. All of a sudden it was *her* house—those were her children and that was her husband. I woke up to someone sobbing and a moment later, I realized that someone was me.

Attempting to stretch the nightmares out of my body, I decided to forgo tanning by the pool and opted for a nice, hot shower instead. Maybe the steam would clear my head.

I got up slowly, stumbled out of bed, and headed for the bathroom. It was just after ten o'clock, so I was confused when I didn't hear Mama moving around downstairs. Once in the bathroom, I found a note from my mother on the mirror that read:

Cora, I'm in the garden. Come join me when you wake up. I'll teach you what to plant this time of year. Love you!

I shook my head and rolled my eyes. Mama loved to garden and was always trying to teach me things. She just couldn't understand why my thumb wasn't green like hers.

As I stepped into the shower and let the warm water run over me, I began to feel better. I took my time, breathing in the steam and releasing all my worries.

Once finished and back in my room, I recalled that Rex would be at my house at two o'clock. I immediately panicked. What would I wear? I didn't want to look like I'd spent hours primping, but I *did* want to look polished. Deciding a white casual sundress would do, I dressed before turning on the blow dryer and styling my hair. When that task was completed, I attempted to cover the pain that was so obvious on my face, only to realize it would take much more than blush and mascara to accomplish such a difficult feat.

I dreaded going outside to see my mother. She would know right away that something was wrong, and I couldn't bear to give her the details. I couldn't bear to *think* about the details. Taking a ragged breath, I straightened my shoulders, raised my chin, and smiled into the mirror. That would just have to suffice.

I left my bedroom and headed down the stairs, through the kitchen, and into the backyard. Once outside, I made my way to the garden where Mama was working. She appraised my outfit and shook her head. She already knew I wasn't planning on learning about flowers that day.

"Well, guess you don't wanna help me out here, do ya, hon?" she asked.

I worded my reply carefully, so she wouldn't suspect anything. "Actually, I thought I'd go shoppin' for a couple of hours. I've been wantin' to redecorate my room, and I need some new curtains and stuff."

"Oh, sounds like fun. Valerie goin' with you?" Mama asked, studying my reaction.

"No, I thought I'd go by myself." I paused, conjuring up a good reason for that. "I mean, ya know, sometimes it's easier to go alone if you know what you're lookin' for. Val and I would probably get distracted and it would take forever." I attempted a chuckle, but it came out all wrong.

That reasoning seemed to please Mama, and she just kept on planting her flowers. "Okay, hon, guess that makes sense. Well, be careful…and stay in town, all right? Don't go too far."

"Sure, Mama." I turned and practically ran toward the house. I couldn't believe I'd escaped so easily! Throwing open the back door, I made my way to the living room, grabbed my purse, and was back outside in no time. I scanned the neighborhood, looking for Rex, but didn't see him. Having no idea where I would even go, I hopped in my car, buckled up, and started the engine.

I'd completely made up the story about redecorating my room. In all honestly, I loved the way my bedroom looked. There was no way out now, though, I'd have to change it. Maybe I'd just get new curtains and rearrange things.

Rock music blasted from my car stereo as I pulled out of the driveway and onto the road. This was my therapy. Characteristically, I enjoyed listening to country or the top hits, but there was something ironically calming about the angry chords and thudding bass of a good, old-school rock song. At this particular moment in my life, anything else would have brought on another melt down, and I was *not* up for that.

I was so lost in thought that I nearly drove past the entry to Suzie's Creations, a local home and garden store. Slamming on the brakes, I peeled into the parking lot, turned off the car, and checked my reflection in the mirror on the sun visor before walking into Suzie's. It was eleven thirty, and I didn't need to be back at home until about one thirty, so I took my time browsing through the store.

I studied the drapery section for a long time, debating between the different curtains. Once I'd chosen a couple, I put them in my shopping cart and headed for the wall décor. I figured it wouldn't hurt to add a few things that would accent the Paris theme of my bedroom. I was examining an antique-looking clock when someone called my name.

"Cora?"

I froze, momentarily panicking. I prayed I wouldn't turn around and see Jeff. It was a male's voice, but I'd been in such a trance that I hadn't recognized it. I turned slowly, my heart racing.

"Landon!" I exclaimed. "Hey! What are you doin' in here?" Even though our friendship was back on track and we'd been spending time together regularly, it had been several days since we'd seen each other because of our extracurricular schedules.

He chuckled at my enthusiasm. "Just pickin' somethin' up for my mom. So how are you?" he asked, looking into my eyes with an intensity that would have forced me to lie if it'd been anyone else.

"Honestly? Not so great. I mean, I *was* fine, but then I found out about Jeff and Lacy's engagement..." I stopped there, knowing I'd said enough. He would understand.

"Yeah, I heard about that," he replied, taking my hand. He stared at me with the sincerest of concern. "I'm sorry, Cora. I know what you must be goin' through. What can I do to help?"

"Oh, I'm fine, really. It's just...hard to swallow. But I'm fine." I had to look away. I'd never been able to lie to him.

Landon didn't argue with me, even though I suspected he knew I was covering up my feelings. "Come here," he said as he embraced me in a tight bear hug. "I'm sorry you have to deal with this. He never deserved you." Landon squeezed me once, then leaned back to look at me. "You know that, right?"

"Sure, that's what I keep hearin'." I sighed. Then I looked into his sweet eyes and said softly, "But thanks, Landon. Really."

"Hey, what are friends for?" He grinned. "It's really good to see you, Cora. I've missed you the past couple weeks. Sorry we haven't hung out as much lately. I've been pretty busy with ball practice."

"That's okay. I'm just glad you're playin' again. I've missed you too, though. We should definitely get together soon," I answered. "Hey, my parents are havin' a party next Saturday. You should come!"

Landon's eyes lit up and a smile stretched all the way across his face. "Sounds great! What time?"

"I think it starts at one, but you know you're welcome whenever." I grinned in return. I couldn't help it, he had a way of making me feel better. Whole.

"Awesome! Count me in," he replied. "Well, I better get this stuff home. I'll see ya next week." He leaned over and kissed my forehead, which was something he'd always done as a key indication of our friendship.

"See ya Saturday, Landon."

I drove home with a new attitude. I was actually happy, or at least headed in that direction. Seeing Landon—even for that brief moment—had lifted my spirits. He was able to do that because he seemed to know just what to say and what not to say. He knew when to ask questions and when to just listen. Next to Valerie, he was my best friend.

He was sort of like my own personal lighthouse—he always helped me find my way home.

CHAPTER EIGHT

Not only did seeing Landon help relax me, but also contributing to my good mood was the anticipation I felt about seeing Rex again. I got home around one thirty, and knew Rex would arrive soon. I had lunch with Mama before heading upstairs to freshen up and wait.

It was almost two o'clock and I was getting nervous. What if he had changed his mind? What if he'd realized how ordinarily plain I was, especially compared to him? I began to worry he wouldn't show—then what would I do? I desperately needed the distraction of a new fling to keep my mind off Jeff and Lacy. Otherwise, I might *actually* go crazy.

A few minutes later, I heard the doorbell ring. I was itching to run downstairs, but didn't want to seem too anxious, like I had nothing better to do with my day than sit around and wait for him.

I heard Mama call my name, so I rushed out of my room to the stairs. I paused at the top, straightening my dress and running a hand through my hair. Boy, I was nervous!

Mustering all the confidence I could manage, I slowly made my way to the living room. As soon as he came into view, I nearly gasped aloud. His beauty was astonishing, completely off the charts. I'd almost forgotten, and seeing him again took my breath away just as it had the first time.

"Hi, Cora" He greeted me with that mesmerizing voice.

"Hello, Rex. How are you today?" *Whoa, that sounded way too formal.* I needed to relax, so I reminded myself to breathe.

"Well, I'll leave you two kids alone. Gotta get back to my gardening," Mama announced. I was relieved she wouldn't be hanging around.

"It was nice to meet you, ma'am," Rex said. "I'll be sure to give this recipe to my mother."

"Thanks, Rex. Tell her she can come by anytime if she wants to chat about some more recipes."

I couldn't believe what I was hearing. Rex had already made a good impression on my mother! That was definitely *not* an easy task for the guys I'd dated. It had taken her a month to warm up to the idea of Jeff and me.

"Sure thing, Ma'am."

She left then and I looked at Rex with raised eyebrows. "Well, my mama seems to like you."

"She's a sweet lady," Rex noted.

"Well, it's good you feel that way. She's usually not so willing to let guys hang out with me."

"You mean she doesn't let you date?" Rex asked with concern. "Because I don't want to break any rules or anything..."

"Oh, no, that's not what I meant. She lets me date. She just usually gives the guy a harder time." I paused as what he'd said about breaking rules registered. "So...you won't need to worry about breaking any rules…if you wanted to…well, date me." I smiled timidly, looking up at him through my eyelashes.

"Well, as long as she's okay with it…are you? Okay with it, I mean, because I'd love to ask you out sometime."

His question made me blush. "Oh, I'm definitely okay with it. You have my permission to ask me out…sometime…if you want," I stammered.

"Cool." He laughed. "In the meantime, I brought a couple of movies over, but I also brought my guitar. I could play some tunes if you'd like." Rex gestured to his left, and I tore my eyes away from his long enough to follow his gaze. Sure enough, a guitar case leaned against the front door.

His guitar! I grinned internally. I was a sucker for guys with guitars. "I'd love to hear you play," I said.

"Awesome," he replied, taking a step to the side and and picking up his guitar. After carefully removing it from the case, he sat down on the couch and began strumming out a rhythm that wasn't familiar to me.

"That's beautiful, Rex. I don't think I've heard it, though," I commented, joining him on the couch.

"That's because I wrote it last night." He paused, gazing intently into my eyes. "For you."

Wow! Blinking, I attempted to regain my composure. "Rex, that's…amazing." I scooted closer to him, inhaling the scent of his cologne, and listened to his beautiful voice singing words meant only for me. I was instantly blown away. "Swept off my feet" would've been the understatement of the century.

After Rex finished playing his latest composition, he asked if there was anything specific I wanted to hear. I mentioned a popular song, and we spent the next two hours discussing our favorite musicians, discovering we had some of the same tastes. We also learned that we had a few *very* different opinions when it came to the subject of country music. Laughing, I tried to convince him to give the genre a try, while he jokingly argued that all country songs were composed of the same themes.

Just as Rex was putting his guitar back into its case a little while later, his phone buzzed. "I hate to do this," he said, "but I have to go. I thought I'd be able to stay longer, but my dad just sent me a text and said he needs my help unloading some new furniture."

"Oh," I answered, disappointed. "Well, that's okay. Thanks for comin' over…I had a lot of fun."

He smiled. "So did I."

We were quiet for a moment, both of us unsure of our next move. Finally, I spoke. "So, the block party my parents are havin' next Saturday…is your family comin'?"

"I don't know if they are. But *I'd* be more than happy to come…if the invitation's open."

"Of course it's open!" I replied a bit too enthusiastically.

"Cool, so I'll see you then," he said. "What time?"

"The fun starts at one."

He leaned in and hugged me, brushing hair away from my shoulder in the process. "I'll see you at one, then. I can't wait."

The next weekend couldn't come soon enough. I went to the mall with Valerie and Kayla after school one day that week, the park with the whole crew another afternoon, and Friday evening was spent helping Mama clean the house to get ready for the party.

When Saturday morning finally arrived, I couldn't contain my excitement. It felt like an eternity since I'd seen Rex, even though in reality it had only been a matter of days.

I was just finishing my makeup when there was a knock on my bedroom door. "Who's there?" I called.

"Hey, Cor, it's Landon. You decent?"

Landon! I stiffened. In all my excitement about Rex, I'd completely forgotten that I had invited Landon to the party, too. What should I do? I hadn't even mentioned Rex to him. And I *definitely* wasn't ready for the two of them to meet.

It doesn't matter, I told myself. *Landon's just a friend. He won't mind that I'm potentially dating someone else. It'll be fine.*

"Um, yeah. Come on in," I answered.

Landon pushed open the bedroom door. "Wow, you look…" He paused as he appraised my cut-off denim mini skirt and hot-pink sleeveless top.

"I look…?" I grinned, teasing him.

"There aren't words, Cora. Even 'beautiful' seems weak compared to the way you look right now."

Whoa. The mascara wand in my hand clattered onto the vanity. I was stunned by his compliment. Blushing, I grabbed the fallen makeup. "I'm such a klutz sometimes," I mumbled.

Landon laughed at my embarrassment. "Sometimes?"

"Very funny. *Any*how, I guess we can go join the party. Daddy should be warmin' the grill up. I'm sure he'd appreciate your help."

"Awesome! It's been forever since I grilled out with your dad!" he exclaimed. He'd always helped my father with the grill when we'd had these parties in the past. They got along well, and Daddy enjoyed the company.

"Come on, I'll walk you down."

We headed downstairs and out the back door to the pool deck. No other guests had arrived, since it was only twelve thirty.

Daddy was excited to see Landon. "Hey!" he called. "My main man! Glad you could come!"

"Me too. Get that grill fired up!"

Once we reached Daddy standing by the grill, he and Landon chatted about guy stuff for a few minutes before I finally interrupted. "Well, you boys have fun. I'm gonna go see if Mama needs any help inside." I waited for a response but got nothing. Shaking my head and thinking about how easily distracted men were, I walked into the kitchen and found Mama mixing some pasta salad.

"Cora, there you are. Could you chop up some carrots for me?"

"Yeah," I replied as I grabbed a knife and cutting board. "Mama, can I ask you a question?"

"Sure, sweetie."

"Well." I hesitated, wondering if I should bring up the subject of Rex again. "I invited Rex to this party."

"Mmm-hmm."

"And I invited Landon."

Mama stopped mixing and looked up from her pasta. "Is that a problem?"

"Well, I don't really know."

She eyed me curiously. "What do you mean? You and Landon are just friends, right?"

"Of course. But I haven't actually told him about Rex yet. I just...I don't know how he'll respond. I kind of forgot that Landon would be here when I invited Rex."

"I see," she said.

I waited. She wasn't giving me much input. Her short answers frustrated me. "Well, what should I do?" I asked impatiently.

"I think you should get Landon alone before Rex gets here. If you truly have no feelings for him stronger than friendship, you need to clarify that. Don't keep leadin' him on, Cora."

Leading him on? Since when did Mama think I was doing that? "Do you really think that's what I'm doin'? I mean, he doesn't have romantic feelings for me, either...I don't think."

"Well, honey, you've spent an awful lot of time with him these past few months. And boys don't always get the hint. You have to be pretty straight forward with them," she replied.

I groaned. "I guess you're right, I should go talk to him. Is this enough carrots?"

She glanced at the few carrots I'd chopped and chuckled. "It's a start. But you go ahead and I'll finish up in here."

"Thanks, Mama." I wiped my hands on a dishtowel, tossed it onto the counter, and headed out the front door since my mother now had the back door blocked by supplies for the party. I didn't even make it to the side of the house before I heard my name.

"Cora!" Rex called.

Oh, no, I thought. I turned to face him as he walked toward me. "Hey, Rex! Thanks for comin'!" I said, smiling to hide my anxiety. Surprisingly, my heart didn't race when he wrapped his arms around my waist and embraced me. Of course I noticed how handsome he looked in his khaki pants and light blue button-up shirt—sleeves rolled up to his elbows, top two buttons undone—and how rock hard his body felt against mine. But my thoughts were too focused on the dreaded conversation with Landon to really *appreciate* these things.

"Sorry I'm a little early." He grinned. "I noticed your dad outside, and I just couldn't wait to see you again."

I blushed and felt a small flutter in my heart at his words—found those butterflies. "I couldn't wait to see you, either." My blush deepened when I realized he still had his arms around the lowest part of my waist. Remembering Landon, I slowly and regretfully shrugged out of Rex's hold.

"Come on out to the deck. I want you to meet a couple of people."

"Sure thing," he answered.

When I turned around, I spotted Landon at the front doorway. I met his gaze and stopped. We both stood frozen, his face rigid with anger.

CHAPTER NINE

After what felt like an eternity, I broke our stare and glanced at Rex, who was observing the interaction curiously. "Um, let's go this way. You can meet Landon," I mumbled, my stomach in nervous knots.

As we approached, Landon's face relaxed a bit. "Hey, Cora, who's your friend?" he asked. Despite his obvious efforts, the words came out through clenched teeth.

"Landon, this is Rex. He just moved in across the street. Rex, this is my friend Landon."

"Pleasure to meet you," Rex said, extending his hand.

Landon took the outstretched hand and shook with a little too much force. "Same here."

"So how do you two know each other?" Rex asked.

"Um, well. We kinda…grew up together, and…ya know…" I trailed off, struggling to answer the question.

"Dated," Landon spat, glaring at Rex. "We dated. And we're still close." The jealousy pouring out of him hit me with a million pounds of force. He was trying to claim his territory, and it bugged me. *He* broke up with *me* all that time ago. Sure, we were great friends, but what right did that give him to intimidate Rex?

I shot him a warning look. "Yeah, we're very close *friends*," I said, emphasizing the last word.

"Right," Landon muttered. "Anyway, I was trying to find you, Cora. Your dad was wonderin' if you have any other guests comin'. He needs to know how many burgers we should make."

"Val, Kayla, and Troy. Mike may or may not show up. Make an extra one for him just in case," I said coldly.

"Fine. I'll let Jack know." Without another word or so much as a glance at Rex, Landon was gone. I fumed internally at the name drop.

"I'm so sorry, Rex," I apologized. "I have no idea what that was all about. He's usually a really nice guy."

Rex chuckled softly. "I'd be pretty bitter too, if I'd let you get away."

I frowned, considering the possibility that Landon may not be angry with me but that he might actually be angry with himself for letting me "get away," as Rex put it. All harsh feelings toward him vanished as I considered the possible weight of his regret.

"Maybe that's what it is. Anyway, let's go out back," I said.

"Sure." Rex draped his arm casually around my shoulder, but instead of feeling giddy, I just felt annoyed. Was he trying to claim *his* territory now? This was getting to be way too much. I silently wished for Kayla and Val to arrive soon.

When they did finally show up half an hour later, with Mike and Troy in tow, I introduced them all to Rex and led them to the food.

"Um, hey, girls…you can put your purses in my bedroom," I said, trying to get them away from the guys so I could vent about my present predicament.

Val seemed to notice the anxiety in my expression, so she took mine and Kayla's arms. "All right, let's go."

"Be right back," Kayla called to Troy over her shoulder.

When we were safely in my room with the door closed, I flung myself down on the bed and sighed in desperation.

"What's wrong?" Val implored.

Kayla sat down beside me. "Yeah, you look like you're about to explode."

I sat up slowly. "I am! So, long story short—" I paused, searching my brain for a starting point to this madness.

Val raised her eyebrows expectantly, waiting for the story. "Well...?" she asked.

"Okay, you both know about this thing with Rex. You both also know that Landon's one of my best friends, and has been for a really long time. Well..." I replayed the previous hour for them, not leaving anything out. Once every detail had been divulged, I huffed and lay all the way back on the bed again.

"Wow," Kayla breathed.

Val grinned. "I told you! I knew it all along. Landon has the hots for you!"

"This is serious, Val," I shrieked. "What am I gonna do?"

"Sorry," she mumbled. "Well, how do you feel about *him*? It's obvious how he feels. I mean, you can't deny it now, Cora. He wouldn't be so jealous if he didn't love you."

I leapt up as if my mattress was made of hot lava. "Love?" I blinked. "What are you talkin' about? Nobody said a *thing* about love!"

"Okay, calm down," Val said. "Geez, I wasn't tryin' to freak you out. I just know Landon's in love with you. He always has been and probably always will be."

"I don't think so, Val. He's just jealous because we've been spendin' so much time together and now he has competition. Typical guy thing. They don't like to share their toys. I'm sure it has more to do with *territory* than love."

Kayla piped in then. "No, Val's right. He's crazy about you. Everybody can see it...except you."

I thought back to Landon's pool party and the kiss we'd shared. It had been months and I still hadn't told my friends. I debated internally about whether or not to spill the beans. There would be no arguing with them once they knew about that kiss.

"Okay, I have to tell y'all somethin'. I've been keepin' this to myself for a really long time because I didn't wanna face it."

Kayla and Valerie glanced at each other and then stared expectantly at me. "What is it, Cora?" Kayla asked.

"Do y'all remember that pool party at London's house, back in September?"

"When that witch, Lacy, showed up? Yeah, I remember," Val muttered.

"What about it?" Kayla inquired.

I quickly rushed through the whole story and then held my breath for their reactions.

Kayla's eyes grew wide. "Seriously? You two *kissed*? I can't believe you didn't tell us!"

"I didn't tell anybody. I wanted to sort it out by myself without any kind of influence. We both decided to forget it ever happened and not let it ruin our friendship."

"No, Cora, *you* decided to forget it ever happened. Landon never forgot."

"What? How do you know?" I questioned, eyeing Val suspiciously.

She touched my arm. "You might wanna sit down for this."

"What?"

"A couple of days ago, Landon and I were talkin' after fourth period and I asked him how he felt about you." She paused to study my reaction. "I'm sorry. I hope you don't think I overstepped my boundaries or somethin'. But I just *had* to know. Y'all've been spendin' so much time together, and I didn't want you to miss out on somethin' that could be great. So I just came right out and asked him."

I wandered over to the chair in front of my vanity and sank down into it. "So...what—"

"He told me about the kiss," Val gushed. "And then he told me he's crazy in love with you. And has been forever."

"What?" A flood of thoughts jumbled my mind and my heart skipped a beat. I couldn't even think straight. I didn't know if I should be happy or angry. I just felt flustered. "Why didn't you tell me?" I demanded.

"I'm so sorry, Cor! He swore me to secrecy. He was plannin' on tellin' you himself...today." She stopped, waiting for my response.

My breath came out in a rush. "Today?" I whispered.

"Yeah..."

Kayla, who'd been listening quietly to Val's revelation, suddenly shrieked with happiness. "Oh, my gosh! This is so great! I always knew you and Landon would get back together. He's perfect for you, and you two make such a cute couple, and now y'all can go to prom together! You'll have the perfect end to senior year, and then you'll go off to college together and then eventually get ma—"

I cut Kayla short, shaking my head. "Stop! Don't you dare finish that sentence! Nobody's gettin' back together, and nobody's even considerin'...*marriage!*"

She bit her lip apologetically. "Maybe I got a little carried away."

"Humph. A little?" I stood, crossed my arms, and narrowed my eyes. "Now, both of you listen to me very carefully. Landon's my *friend*. Nothin' more. I'll have to talk to him about his feelings, of course, but we *won't* be gettin' back together. We've been down that road and it obviously didn't work out. I'd rather have his friendship than risk losin' it just so we can have an excuse to make out. I'm sure he'll see my point of view. So, please, just drop it."

"You won't even consider this? Sleep on it?" Val pushed.

"No."

Kayla let her shoulders slump in defeat. "Well, in that case, you'd better get him alone so you can reject him in private...before he embarrasses himself any more today."

Val glanced at Kayla and then let out a deep breath to emphasize her disappointment. "Should we go get him for you? It's probably better to have that conversation up here, where you won't be interrupted."

"Yeah, guess I might as well get it over with," I answered, toying with a necklace strewn across my vanity. Those knots were in my stomach again, and I was so distracted that I didn't even notice my friends leave. I stared at myself in the mirror, wondering how I'd let things get so messed up.

Moments later, a sudden knock startled me back to reality. Landon cracked open the door, peeking his head in. "Cora?"

I glanced up at him and bit my lip out of nervous habit. "Hey, Landon."

"The girls said you wanted to talk to me," he said quietly. Then his words were coming out in a rush. "Look, I'm real sorry about the way I acted out there. You know, with that Rex kid. I didn't mean to be such a jerk. It's just that when I saw him hug you...well, I felt like the breath had been knocked out of me. I've been meanin' to tell you somethin' for a while now, and I don't wanna put it off anymore. It's important, and it's all I think about these days—"

"Landon, please don't say anything else." I closed my eyes, sucked in a deep breath for courage, and opened them to stare at his sweet face. I exhaled slowly, and began letting him down as gently as I could. "Listen, I know how you feel about me," I began. "Val told me what you said to her. I'm real flattered, Landon, but I don't think it's actually love, ya know? I mean, we've been spendin' a lot of time together and we've gotten to be pretty close again. The way we used to be, before we were a couple. I think, maybe, what you feel is more of a...I don't know...territorial thing. It's not really love, Landon."

He stared at me, incredulous—perhaps too shocked to move. It was a long time before he finally spoke. "I...can't...believe you," he said slowly. He shook his head and huffed, "You're so stubborn, you know that? You're the most stubborn girl I ever met. And how do you know what's goin' on in *my* head? Or my heart? What makes you so sure about how *I* feel?"

I cringed, hoping he wouldn't let his temper get the best of him. The last thing I wanted to do was make him mad. "Please don't get upset, Landon. I'm not tryin' to hurt you or insult you. I just don't want this to go on any longer...I'm afraid we'll lose what we have. And I don't want that. It's too special."

"I really wish you'd quit with that 'we'll lose what we have' stuff. It's a bad excuse. Why don't you just come right out and say it? You're not attracted to me."

I winced at his response. How could he think I wasn't attracted to him, after all we'd been through? "You couldn't be more wrong!" I snapped. "If I wasn't attracted to you, why would I have *ever* dated you? And why would I have let you kiss me at your pool party? I don't make it a habit to go around kissin' random guys, Landon."

His anger vanished instantly and he grinned. "So you *are* attracted to me. Then what's the problem?" he asked nonchalantly.

I groaned. "Ugh! You're not listenin' to me!"

"Yes, I am," he replied. "But all I'm hearin' are excuses, not reasons. Give me one good *reason* we shouldn't be together. And don't say because it'd ruin our friendship."

"Well, I..."

"You?"

Suddenly I jumped out of the chair I'd been sitting in and threw my hands up in the air. "I don't know! Okay? Is that what you wanted to hear?"

He took a step toward me. "If that's the truth, then, yes, it's exactly what I wanna hear."

"I don't know what the truth *is*. I just don't think it's a good idea for us to get back together. That's it. End of discussion."

He recoiled as if I'd slapped him across the face. "What are you so scared of?"

I rolled my eyes and took a few steps away from him. "I'm not scared of anything, Landon. I just don't wanna talk about this anymore. Besides, Rex is out there waitin' for me."

"Oh, I see how it is," he grumbled. "You got a new boy now, so you won't even consider what I'm askin'."

"Landon, come on. Don't—"

"No," he interrupted. "Look, Cora, this is how it's gonna be. This thing—whatever we've been doin'—it's gonna stop. From now on, it's all or nothin'."

My heart dropped to the floor. "What are you sayin'?"

"I'm sayin' it's him or me. We either do this all the way or not at all."

I swallowed, holding back tears. "That's pretty harsh, Landon."

"No, what's harsh is bein' strung along for months, thinkin' there's hope when there's really not. I gave you up to somebody else before, and I can't go through that again. So tell me right now what it's gonna be."

My lips quivered, but I managed to stutter, "I can't...please don't make me choose."

He stared at me with a blank expression. "I guess that's my answer," he mumbled. Then he spun around and strode out of my bedroom—and my life.

CHAPTER TEN

The cool morning air whipped across my face as I jogged the remaining few feet back to my driveway. After the big fight with Landon—which was three weeks ago and we *still* hadn't spoken—I needed a change in my life. Because cheerleading was over for the season, I felt like I should do something to stay in shape.

One Sunday afternoon, I read an article about the numerous health benefits of running, and the decision was made. I'd been running every weekday morning since. It fulfilled my craving for a fresh start and had the benefit of keeping me in shape. Despite my characteristic reluctance to get out of bed in the mornings, I loved running. Once my body became accustomed to the early rise and the exertion of energy, it was actually relaxing. I loved how fresh the air felt at that time of day and how peaceful our neighborhood was before the residents were out and about.

I slowed to a walk and smiled as I took in the sound of birds chirping and the scent of freshly cut grass. Although things weren't completely right—Landon was avoiding me, not even hanging out with our friends if I was going to be around—I was making an effort to live every day to the fullest. With only a month of high school left, I wanted to take advantage of every get together with friends, every pep rally, every sleep over, and every date with Rex—especially prom.

The big night was exactly one week and one day away. Next Saturday, I'd be spinning around the dance floor in a beautiful dress with Rex by my side.

Back inside the house, I stared at my prom dress while I threw on a pair of jeans and a tank top, and while I fixed my hair, and while I put on makeup. Excitement flooded through me every time I looked at that dress. It was a glittering, bright pink fabric, long and fitted with a halter neck, and flowing out slightly at the bottom. It was the perfect dress for what I hoped would be the perfect night.

Prom was still on my mind when I pulled into my assigned parking space at school later that morning. I was contemplating whether to wear my hair up or down when a knock on my window startled me back to the present reality.

Val stood outside my car and glanced impatiently at her watch while I grabbed my purse and books. "We're gonna be late for homeroom! What in the world were you doin' just sittin' there?"

"Sorry, I was thinkin' about prom and stuff," I replied apologetically.

"Ugh, don't remind me," she grumbled. "If I don't find a date soon—like today—I won't even be goin'. And then I'll have to return my dress!"

"You're *not* gonna return your dress," I assured her for the millionth time. "Somebody'll ask you." Personally, I couldn't figure out why nobody *had* asked her yet. She was sweet, pretty, and fun.

"Nope, afraid not." She sighed. "I just have to face it: all the good guys are taken. It's senior year, most people are in relationships. I have no boyfriend, so…no prom date."

It was true that Valerie wasn't in a serious relationship, but she'd been on a lot of dates—guys were always asking her to go out with them. Unfortunately, most of those guys had gone on to find somebody they could call their girlfriend, however short-lived. Val simply wasn't the exclusive relationship type. She always claimed having that kind of commitment in high school would only lead to disappointment. Which I now knew to be true.

We were silent as we walked through the parking lot, into the school, and down the hall toward class. Finally, I tried one more push. "Why don't *you* just ask somebody? After all, it *is* the twenty-first century. Aren't women allowed to make the first move these days?"

We pushed through the door to our homeroom and she tossed her books onto a desk in the back. "Well, yeah, but who would I ask? Everybody's already *got* a date. I can't believe this is happenin' to me!" she whined, plopping down in her seat.

"It'll be okay, Val. You'll find somebody great to go with, and we'll all have an awesome time! Don't stress. I'll help you think of somethin'. I promise."

"You're so lucky to have Rex. You get to go to prom with a hot college guy."

"He's not *actually* a college guy," I replied in an attempt to make her feel better. While it was true that Rex had already graduated high school, he was taking a year off to decide what he wanted to do with his life.

Valerie rolled her eyes. "Close enough." The history teacher entered the room then, so our conversation was cut short as we took out our books and began to listen to a lecture on the role of secret agents during WWII.

After a long day of learning about wars, chloroplasts, narcissistic personality disorder, and other information that would supposedly be helpful to my future, I met Val and Kayla by the lockers. I grabbed the books I would need for homework and hurriedly shoved the rest into my locker. When the others had done the same, we headed out to the student parking lot. As we neared the senior lot, a strange thing happened.

"Cora!"

I turned slowly at the sound of my name being called. The voice was a little too familiar.

Jeff stood a few feet back from us, his body twisted halfway around, like he was ready to bolt at a moment's notice.

"What do *you* want?" I spat. It was the first time we'd spoken to each other since the mortifying incident in the cafeteria. I'd wondered how I would react to him if given the chance. Now I knew.

"Um, I was wonderin' if we could talk in private." He seemed nervous. I'd never seen him so uneasy.

"Whatever you have to say to me, you can say in front of Valerie and Kayla. You should know that."

He sighed. "Please, Cora? This would be a lot easier for me if we were alone."

"And why should I make this easier for you? You sure haven't made things *easy* for me," I retorted, rolling my eyes.

He looked at the ground. When his eyes met mine again, they were full of something unrecognizable—regret, maybe? "I know. That's what I wanna talk to you about."

"Oh," I said stupidly. I was stumped. Was he attempting to apologize?

"Yeah, so…" He trailed off as if waiting for me to make the next move.

"Um, okay…go ahead and talk then," I finally stammered.

Valerie jumped in before Jeff could start his speech. "Kay, let's give these two some privacy," she said.

"Right," Kayla answered, following Val to her car.

As I watched them walk away, I noticed that the sky, which had been bright blue not more than ten minutes ago, was suddenly hazy. A huge, dark cloud hovered above us. It felt strangely ominous, perhaps because it was reminiscent of the weather on the day I'd caught Jeff and Lacy together. Ironic.

"Listen, Cora, I...well, I don't even know where to start," Jeff huffed and sat down, leaning against a tree. He patted the spot next to him. "Sit with me."

I hesitated. He was being too friendly now. Apparently, he'd relaxed a good bit since the girls had left. I took a deep breath and carefully sat on the soft grass that separated the rows of parking spots, leaving a foot of space between us.

"Maybe you should start with why you're all of a sudden so interested in talkin' to me," I suggested.

"I wanna apologize. What I did to you was wrong and I never meant for you to get hurt."

"Ha. Maybe you should've thought of that *before* you sucked face with Lacy." We were silent for a long time. The wind grew stronger with each passing second. A storm was definitely brewing.

"I know I shouldn't have done what I did. Trust me, I know. And I didn't mean for it to happen. She wouldn't give up. She kept throwin' herself at me. Every day, she flirted with me 'til I finally gave in. I'm only human, Cora."

"You're *only* human? That's your excuse?" I exclaimed, jumping to my feet. "Ugh, you make me sick, Jeffrey Colton!"

He stood too. "That didn't come out right. What I meant was I'm human and I make mistakes, and I made a huge mistake with you. I messed up what we had…and for no good reason. I don't even care about her."

I gaped wide-eyed at him. "You don't care about her? I'm sorry, that seems a little odd since you two are *engaged*."

He shook his head. "That's what I'm tryin' to tell you. We're *not* engaged. It's a rumor Lacy started after I dumped her. I don't know if she was tryin' to get back at me or get me back. Either way, we're not engaged. We're not even together."

I had to take a step back to steady myself. I could feel the shock frozen on my face. *He's not engaged. He's not engaged.* No matter how many times I thought it, I couldn't bring myself to believe it. All the tears I'd wasted and the sleepless nights I'd spent because of their "engagement" were in vain.

"You're not…together?" I whispered.

Jeff stepped forward, closing the gap between us, and took my hand. "No, we're not. I don't love her." He paused, and then brushed his free hand across my cheek. "I love *you*, Cora."

I stepped back again and pulled my hand out of his hold. I couldn't believe my ears. I was at a loss for words. "Jeff, I don't know what to say. I—"

"Say you still love me too, baby," he interrupted.

Closing my eyes, I put a hand over my face. "I'm sorry, Jeff. I can't do that."

He moved my hand so that he could look into my eyes. "You don't feel nothin' at all for me anymore?"

I pondered his question carefully before responding. I searched my head and my heart and found nothing. The only thing I felt was surprise at his confession. I wasn't giddy and there were no butterflies in my stomach. My pulse didn't quicken and I didn't feel flustered the way I used to when he gazed into my eyes. I couldn't believe it. I was completely over Jeff. I almost laughed out loud with relief at that realization.

"No, I don't," I replied in astonishment. "I really don't. I mean, I've always wondered what would happen if I got a second chance with you. I used to dream about this very moment—I wished for it every day. But now...nothin'."

His face crumpled. He actually looked a little pathetic. His usual egotistical attitude completely vanished. "Really? After all that time we were together, and now you're just over me? Just like that?"

"I really *am* sorry," I said softly. "But what you did...well, you hurt me pretty bad. It took a long time for me to get over it, to get over you. But I finally have. Besides, even if I did have feelings for you, I don't think it'd be a good idea for us to date again. I'd have a hard time trustin' you, and trust is the most important thing in a relationship."

He closed his eyes briefly. "I guess I get that. Man, I really screwed up."

"Yeah, but listen...thanks for apologizin'."

He snorted. "Sure."

"No, really. I think we both needed this closure. And it took a lot of courage for you to admit all this to me. So thank you."

"I just didn't want us to graduate without you ever knowin' the truth."

I smiled sympathetically. "Well, I'm glad you told me. I'll see ya around." I reached up to peck him on the cheek, and he wrapped his arms around my waist to pull me into a hug. I allowed myself to hug him back for a minute, inhaling the scent of his cologne for what I assumed would be the last time ever.

"I won't give up, Cora. I know somewhere deep down, there's still somethin' there for me."

"Jeff, no. Don't do that to yourself."

"Don't worry about me." With that, he released his hold on me and spun around. I watched as he walked away.

There was a strange feeling in the pit of my stomach. For some reason I couldn't grasp, I felt uneasy.

CHAPTER ELEVEN

The week flew by. Before I realized it, prom stared me right in the face. I should have been excited, elated. I finally had closure with Jeff, and Rex would accompany me to the biggest night of my life. But through all the planning and all the anticipation, I couldn't escape the nagging feeling that something was wrong or that I was missing something important. Most of the time, I brushed this feeling off, convincing myself it was just nerves. But the night before prom, I was forced to face what I'd been avoiding.

We were sitting down to dinner when Mama took me by surprise. "So have you talked to Landon lately?" she asked, completely out of the blue.

"Um…no. Why do you ask?" I twirled my fork around in the spaghetti in front of me, dodging her gaze.

"Well, I know you two had a bit of a fallin' out at our party a while back, and I haven't heard you mention him. You haven't seen him outside of school since then?" She tried to sound nonchalant, but I could tell there was a motive to her questioning.

"No, I haven't. It's kinda hard, since I'm datin' Rex. I can't exactly drop him to go hang out with a buddy."

"I see," she replied. Her forehead crinkled slightly, and I knew there was something she wanted to say.

"What is it, Mama?" I huffed, waiting for the lecture.

"I ran into his mother today."

"That's nice. How is she?"

"She's fine, but she says Landon's not doin' very well. That he misses you. He's really hurtin' right now, Cora, and I think you should talk to him."

The fork I held slipped through my fingers and clattered noisily onto my plate. "I *have* talked to him, Mama. He won't listen to anything I say. He's just…he's…stubborn." I felt my face flush in frustration and embarrassment. I didn't want to have this conversation with her, especially not in front of my father.

"What are you two women jabberin' about? Is there something goin' on with you and Landon?" Daddy asked. He didn't know anything about the situation.

"No, Daddy. There's nothing goin' on. He's just confused."

Mama chimed in. "Now, Cora, don't dismiss this so easily. He's havin' a real hard time and it's because of you. Even if you didn't hurt him on purpose, you *did* hurt him. That's somethin' you need to face. Do the responsible thing, sweetie. Talk to him and make it right."

I pushed away from the table, scraping my chair against the wooden floor. "I *can't* make it right, Mama. I've tried…believe me, I've tried. There's no reasonin' with him. What do you want from me?" I stood up and grabbed my plate. "I'm sorry, but I've suddenly lost my appetite. Excuse me." I tossed the plate in the sink and stormed out of the dining room, stomping as loudly as possible up the steps. In typical teenage drama-queen fashion, I slammed my bedroom door.

I lay on the bed in the dark, thinking about Landon "not doing very well." The longer I stayed that way—not moving and drowning in self-pity—the worse I felt about my temper tantrum. Slowly, the realization hit that it wasn't my mother I was angry with, it was me.

"Ugh," I groaned. Now I had to apologize to my parents. If not, I'd be guilt-ridden for days.

Jogging downstairs, I sucked in a deep breath for courage. Admitting faults was never easy for me. Unfortunately, it was something I'd become accustomed to lately because of my short temper, which I blamed on raging teenage hormones.

My parents were watching the nightly news when I entered the family room.

"Mama, Daddy…" I hesitated.

"What is it, Cora?" my father asked without taking his eyes off the television.

They weren't going to make this easy for me. "I just wanna apologize for the way I acted earlier," I said quickly.

Daddy looked at me then. "Well, good," he said. "Cuz that kind of behavior's not very ladylike. And I know your mama and I raised you to be a lady, now didn't we?"

"Yes, sir." It wasn't the only time I'd heard this speech.

"All right, then. Now I think you should apologize directly to your mother."

Mama glanced my way for the first time since the conversation had started. Characteristically, she let Daddy take care of punishment or lectures if he was home.

"Sorry I lost my temper, Mama," I mumbled.

She smiled sympathetically. "It's okay, sweetie. I was your age once, you know."

I smiled in return as she gave me one of those all-knowing looks. My smile was only skin-deep, though. Despite the apology, I still felt sick with guilt. And it had absolutely nothing to do with my parents.

Saturday morning—prom morning—dawned gray and dreary. The menacing sky sent a shiver down my spine as I gazed out the window. I prayed the rain would hold off at least until we got to the prom.

Shaking off the eerie sensation, I picked up my cell and called Valerie. She, Kayla, and I planned on getting our nails and hair done together.

"Hey! Can you believe it's the day of our senior prom? It's actually here. I'm so excited! I couldn't even sleep last night!" Val gushed when she answered my call.

Her enthusiasm was contagious, and despite the gray sky and threatening clouds, I squealed in excitement. "I know! I can't believe this is really the day!"

She laughed. "I'm so glad I found a date!"

I'd finally convinced her, after much persuading, to ask somebody to go with her instead of waiting to be asked. To my surprise, she'd decided on Mike—as in Lacy's ex-boyfriend, Mike.

"He just seems like a fun date. And I know he doesn't have anybody to go with since he'd always planned on takin' Lacy," she'd explained when I had questioned her choice. Her answer had pacified me, so I'd dropped the subject.

"Cora?" Val interrupted my thoughts, bringing me back to the present.

"What? Oh, sorry. Yeah, we'll meet at the salon at eleven. That should give us plenty of time. I'll call Kayla."

"Cool. See ya then!"

After I called Kayla to confirm the time with her, I took a quick shower and threw on some jeans and a button-up shirt—so as not to mess up my hair once it was done—and headed down the stairs. I didn't make it out the door before Mama stopped me.

"Oh, Cora! Pause for a picture, sweetie! I can't believe you're goin' to prom tonight! Your senior prom... Oh, honey you're growin' up so fast!" she cried.

I moaned. "Mama, no pictures yet, please! I don't even have my face on." She ignored my request, clicking picture after picture while I walked through the house. She even took pictures as I got into my car. This was going to be a long day.

"Have fun! I'll see you when you get back!" she called after me.

Fifteen minutes later, I was outside the salon with Kayla and Valerie. As soon as we walked in, we were directed to three adjacent chairs to have our hair styled. I chose to wear mine down with curls, Kayla chose to wear hers in a classic up do, and Val chose a classy side pony. When our hair was done, we sat and gossiped while receiving mani-pedis.

Once our hair and nails were as perfect as we thought possible, my friends and I headed back to my house to finish getting ready. Our dates would meet us there at five o'clock for pictures. Since there was a gazebo outside and my mother took such pride in her gardening, our yard made a beautiful backdrop. At six o'clock, the limo would pick us up and take us to dinner at Manhattan's, which was the nicest restaurant in town, and then we'd head to our high school's gym for the prom.

That was the plan. Of course, nothing ever goes exactly as planned.

"You look beautiful," Rex said when I entered the family room at five o'clock on the dot. The other girls followed right behind me, and Troy stood waiting with Rex. All the parents were there too, standing around and chatting about how quickly kids grow up.

I blushed. "Thanks."

He walked over and kissed me lightly on the cheek. "Oops, hope I didn't mess up your face," he said, realizing his possible mistake.

"No, you're fine," I answered shyly. It felt strange having him show affection in front of my parents.

"Um…where's Mike?" Val asked, her forehead crinkled with worry.

Troy forced his eyes off Kayla for the first time since she'd entered the room. "Don't worry, I just talked to him. He's on his way."

Val exhaled. "Whew, I was startin' to think he was gonna stand me up." As if on cue, there was a knock on the front door. My mother went to answer it and a few minutes later, Mike walked into the family room.

"Hey, y'all, sorry I'm late. Whoa, you girls look awesome." He grinned. Mike always said whatever was on his mind, it was part of the reason we all liked him so much.

"Thanks," we replied in unison.

I glanced around the crowded room. Excitement filled the air. I could almost *feel* the anticipation and anxiety. Some of the moms were starting to tear up, blotting their eyes before any makeup smeared. The dads puffed their chests out with pride as they compared the accomplishments of their kids.

"Excuse me, everybody," I called above the chatter. "We should probably start pictures now that we're all here."

Mama grabbed her camera and raised one hand. "Okay, y'all follow me out to the garden!" For the next half hour, the six of us smiled and posed as our parents took pictures, rearranged us, and took more pictures. I thought my cheeks would fall off by the time we finished.

"My face is numb," Kayla whispered as we made our way back inside.

"I know. Thank goodness that's over!" Val agreed.

"Hey, y'all," I interrupted. "It's a few minutes after six and the limo's not here yet. Should we be worried?" There was really no point for me to ask that question. I was already worried.

Rex joined the conversation. "I'm sure it's fine, beautiful. We'll give him a few more minutes. It's only five after, we have plenty of time."

"Yeah," Mike chimed in. "Our reservation at the restaurant's not 'til 6:30, and it only takes a few minutes to get there."

Kayla frowned. "It kinda sucks they're not here yet, though. We wanted some pictures in front of the limo, and now we may not have time."

Twenty minutes later, my mother was frantic. "I'm gonna go call the limo company," she informed us. "Maybe the driver had a flat tire or somethin'."

Chaos immediately ensued. People were talking over each other, discussing possible reasons the limo hadn't yet arrived. Everybody had their own opinions. Some parents were angry, others worried. Val, Kayla, and I were trying our best not to freak out. A teenage girl's prom was supposed to be perfect—problems led to frustration and tears. The guys attempted to make us feel better with promises that we'd still have a great night and that nothing was ruined.

"I can't get an answer on the phone," Mama announced a few minutes later when she came back into the room. "I can't believe this!"

"The kids need to leave now or they won't have time to eat," Val's mom said with frustration.

"What are we gonna do?" Val exclaimed.

Troy's mother spoke up. "They can take my van. It'll hold everyone."

Great, a minivan for prom, I thought with disgust. But it was better than missing dinner.

Voices grew loud again as other parents volunteered their vehicles for us to use. Finally, I nudged Mama. "Can you get this under control?" I pleaded, on the verge of an emotional breakdown. I just wanted to get to prom.

"Everybody, calm down!" Mama called above the noise. "It makes the most sense for them to use Mrs. Kraman's van, since it's the biggest and she volunteered first." She paused, glancing at Troy's mother. "Are you sure you don't mind?"

"Of course I'm sure!"

"Good, it's settled then. Outside, kids. Let's go." She pushed us toward the door and we rushed to the van. People took more pictures as we piled in—the girls careful not to rip dresses or mess up hair. Then we were off.

Half an hour later, the guys waited at our table while Val, Kayla, and I primped in the restroom of Manhattan's.

"You okay?" Val asked me. "You seem kinda distracted. Are you not havin' a good time?"

I mustered a smile. "Sure, I'm havin' a lot of fun."

Kayla and Val exchanged a look, and then Kayla said, "Come on, Cora. What's wrong?"

I turned away from the mirror and leaned against the cool marble counter. "I just...I don't know what it is, but I feel like somethin's not right. This should be the best night of my life, but for some reason I'm not as happy as I thought I'd be."

"Do you think it has anything to do with Landon?" Kayla asked quietly.

"Yeah, I think so," I responded. "As much as I hate to admit it, it does. Not that I'd rather be here with him or anything. It's just that he's my best friend besides y'all, and I can't even hang out with him at my senior prom. We're not even on speakin' terms. Before long, we'll graduate and I'll be off to New York. We'll lose touch forever. I just...I wish...I don't know what I wish."

Val put her arm around my shoulders. "Remember what you said at the beginning of the year? About this bein' the best prom ever...no drama, right?" She paused and I nodded. "Look, I know you're upset about your fight with Landon, but he'll come around. You two *will* be friends again. There's no question about that. So tonight, put him out of your mind and try to have fun. I promise it'll be okay."

"You're right. I know you're right. Besides, it's not fair to Rex. He deserves all my attention. Which makes me feel even worse...I feel guilty for hurtin' Landon, and then I feel guilty for thinkin' about that while I'm with Rex. Ugh," I groaned. My friends glanced at each other again, and I couldn't tell if their expressions were sympathetic or annoyed.

"I'm sorry, y'all," I apologized. "Enough of my drama. Let's go back out there and have a good time. No more Landon talk for the rest of the night."

"Are you sure you're good?" Kayla asked hesitantly.

"Yeah, I'm fine....just needed to get that off my chest. Thanks for listenin'."

"Anytime. Now let's get back to our dates!" Val said enthusiastically. We all linked arms, pushed through the ladies' room door, and walked back to our table, Kayla and Val giggling the whole time. Mentally, I vowed to be as carefree and happy as the two of them for the rest of the evening.

"Y'all sure took a long time in there," Mike joked as we reoccupied our seats.

"Sorry, my fault. I, uh, had a...makeup emergency," I replied with forced nonchalance.

Rex leaned over and whispered in my ear, "You're gorgeous," causing me to blush and grin—like a silly schoolgirl with a crush.

The rest of dinner went smoothly. I put Landon out of my head, as Val had suggested, and focused on having a good time with my friends. Rex was a perfect gentleman, pulling out my chair when I stood, holding the door for me when we left the restaurant, and helping me into the van. He whispered sweet compliments in my ear all the way to the school, and I ate up every minute of it. The night had completely turned around, becoming magical and romantic like I'd always dreamed.

The gym décor was breathtaking. The bleachers were pushed in, and tables formed a semicircle in which the middle of the floor was left open for dancing. Covering the tables were pale lilac tablecloths with beautiful white roses as centerpieces. White lights lined the walls and hung from the ceiling, shimmering off the pink sparkles of my dress. There was a DJ booth set up on stage, where a red carpet led the way to a decorated podium designated for the crowning of Prom King and Queen. I was in a fairytale as I glided toward the dance floor on Rex's arm.

Rex and I twirled around the floor during a couple of slow songs before the DJ decided to liven things up with faster, hip-hop music. Then we joined Val and Mike and danced to a few hit list songs. Kayla and Troy sat at a table—caught up in the atmosphere of romance—whispering and gazing into each other's eyes. Kayla wasn't much of a dancer, she claimed to have two left feet.

"Whew, I'm wiped. These feet need a break," Val huffed. "I need some punch."

"I'll get it," Mike said.

Val grinned at me and raised her eyebrows. "Thanks, Mike."

"Are you thirsty, beautiful?" Rex whispered in my ear.

"Yeah, thanks. We'll wait for you at the table." He and Mike headed to the back of the gym for the punch while Val and I sat down with Kayla and Troy.

"Hey, you two love birds! Havin' fun yet?" Val asked with a wink.

Kayla giggled and blushed. "Yeah, it's been a great night so far."

I nudged her elbow and smiled mischievously. "You know we're gonna get you out on that dance floor before it's all said and done, right?" I joked.

"No way!" she exclaimed. "I *really* can't dance! Please don't torture me like that!"

"Don't worry, we will." Val chuckled. "You might as well go ahead and get your torture shoes on."

Kayla groaned and we all laughed. Just as I was getting lost in the light-hearted conversation going on around me, I caught sight of Landon dancing with a cute girl in the middle of the floor. He twirled and spun her, and she clung to him as closely as humanly possible, pressing her tiny body against his every chance she got.

CHAPTER TWELVE

My heart stopped and I froze. I felt myself staring, but couldn't tear my eyes away from the scene. And they were definitely making a scene. It was as though they'd rehearsed their routine with a professional. He even lifted her at the end of the song. Applause erupted as the music faded.

How had I not noticed them earlier? Was I that carried away in my own world, my own perfect evening, not to see Landon with her? Or had they just arrived?

I couldn't answer these questions. I couldn't process what was happening or what I was feeling. The stab of pain in my gut felt oddly familiar—like jealousy—but that was ridiculous. I was enjoying my night, my date, and my friends. I was happy. So why did the sight of Landon with that girl send me into mental hysterics?

Something sharp pressed down on my foot, and I realized it was Val's heel. "Get a grip," she whispered. "Rex is headed this way, and he's already watchin' you. Quit lookin' at them…and laugh or somethin'."

Uh-oh. I turned my head toward her dramatically and faked a giggle. "Was I that obvious?" I mumbled through a grin.

"Just keep laughin'," she urged.

A few short moments later, Rex was in the chair next to me with his arm draped over my shoulders. He proceeded to kiss my cheek, as if he were showing off or trying to make a point. Either way, it frustrated me.

I pushed away from the table. "I'm goin' to the ladies' room," I announced. Rex stared after me, dumbfounded. I could feel everyone watching me as I walked away. I didn't care, though. I needed some space. I strode faster toward the restrooms, bumping into a few people on the way. I finally reached my destination and pushed through the door. Once inside, I exhaled and leaned against the wall. Luckily, I was alone.

All I needed was a few minutes to regain control of my emotions and then I'd be fine. Inhaling, I turned to look in the full-length mirror. As the air rushed out of my lungs, I noticed the strained expression on my face. I took a few more deep breaths and tried to smile. It didn't look convincing, so I lifted my chin and tried again. That one was a little better. It would have to do. I stood there for about two more minutes, taking in my appearance.

I realized for the first time how amazing my dress looked. It hugged my curves in all the right places and showed some skin where needed. Bangs swept in an angle across my forehead, and curls brushed the tops of my shoulders. To my surprise, none of the curls had fallen out, despite all the dancing I'd already done. After looking in the mirror, I felt confident enough to face prom night again, no matter what happened.

I'd ignore Landon and his new friend. I'd dance with Rex and let his compliments and sweet gestures sweep me back into my fairytale evening. With that thought, I made my way slowly back to my friends, back to the perfect night of ten minutes ago.

When I approached the table, Rex stood and took my hand. "We need to talk," he whispered. "Come dance with me." A slow song began, and as far as everyone else was concerned, he and I were just going to dance. I appreciated his discretion but dreaded the looming conversation.

Once we moved to a somewhat private spot on the dance floor, Rex put his arms around my waist and pulled me close. We swayed back and forth for a while, but tension hovered in the air between us.

After what seemed like forever, he finally broke the silence. "So...is it all you hoped for?"

"What?" I asked.

"Prom. Tonight."

I managed to smile, praying it looked genuine. "It's been wonderful, Rex. Thank you for everything." As I said the words I knew they were true, even though my heart screamed conflicting messages. It really *had* been a great night, and Rex had done everything he could to make it perfect. He'd even surprised me with a dozen pink roses—my favorite—when he arrived at my parents' house.

"Cora, if I ask you something, do you promise to answer truthfully?"

I stopped swaying and stared into his eyes. I had an idea of the question he wanted to ask, and I didn't want to answer it. I didn't know how. "Of course," I replied softly.

"Well..." He hesitated.

"What's wrong, Rex?"

He averted his eyes briefly, then met my gaze. "Would you rather be here with Landon?"

I blinked slowly and thought of how to word my response. "No, Rex. I'm glad I'm here with you. I'm sorry if I've been distracted tonight. It's just that...this thing with Landon does have me a little upset. But it's not what you think."

He frowned. "Then what is it?"

"Well, he's one of my best friends. We grew up together and now we're not even talkin'. I just hate that I can't hang out with him at our senior prom. I mean, not as a date, but...as a friend. Does that make sense?"

"Yeah, sort of..."

"Is there somethin' else?" I inquired.

"Actually, there is...it's just that I saw your face when he was dancing with that girl. I thought you'd lose it. It didn't seem like the face of someone who just misses her friend. It seemed more like the face of someone who's plagued with jealousy and longing."

"What? No, I-I'm not jealous," I stammered. "And I'm definitely not *longing*. You misread my expression. I was just shocked because I didn't know he was datin' anybody. It was just a surprise. That's what you saw on my face—surprise, not jealousy."

"So you're telling me that you don't have feelings for him? At all? Because I want you to be happy." He brushed his fingers lightly across my cheek, and then held my chin in his hand. "I refuse to be the reason you don't find true love."

"Rex, what are you sayin'? Are you...breakin' up with me?" I whispered.

"No, I'm not. Unless...unless it's what *you* want. I'm crazy about you...I'm in love with you."

Whoa. We hadn't said the "L" word yet. I had no idea we were at that point in our relationship. It felt rushed. I took an involuntary step back, but Rex didn't release his hold on my waist.

"I love you, Cora," he murmured. "Do you love me?"

I looked deep into his eyes, remembering the spark I'd felt the first day I met him, and the times we'd spent together since. My eyes searched his face, but all I found was an attractive guy. A guy so attractive he could be a model, but that was all I saw.

In that moment I realized that everything I felt for him was superficial. I was crazy about him because of his looks, and because he knew how to romance me. I'd gotten so carried away in his grand gestures—like the song he had written for me—that I'd lost *myself*. I was infatuated with his voice and his charm, but I wasn't in love with him. And I hadn't expected to face that fact so soon.

Wow.

I closed my eyes and inhaled, then slowly let my breath out. "No. I'm sorry, Rex."

His face fell and he dropped his arms. "Oh."

I took his hand and met his stare. "Don't get me wrong, I really like you. And I've had a lot of fun hangin' out…I just don't think I can *honestly* say I'm in love with you. Not yet, it's too soon. I'm so, so sorry."

He smiled wistfully and touched my cheek again. "It's okay, we haven't known each other that long. But I'm a firm believer that when you know, you know. I do wish you felt differently, but I don't think you ever will. Your heart's somewhere else, so I'm going to bow out gracefully."

I blinked back tears. Even though I knew he was right and that we shouldn't keep going down this path to nowhere, it hurt to see our relationship end. "I'll miss you," I whispered.

"Me too," he said. Then he turned to leave.

"Wait! How will you get home?"

"I'll take a taxi. Don't worry about me, Cora. I'll be okay."

"Are you sure? Because you're more than welcome to stay. We can still hang out tonight…I don't want you to feel like you have to go."

He took a few steps back toward me. "I don't belong here. This is *your* night. Go find your happiness, Cora. And don't be stubborn," he said sincerely. "Good-bye, beautiful." He kissed my cheek and started toward the exit again. I watched as he disappeared in the crowd.

I don't know how long I stood there before Val's voice startled me out of my own thoughts. "What're you doin'? Where's Rex?" she asked anxiously.

"He's gone. We broke up," I answered in a monotone voice, still staring at the spot where he'd disappeared.

"What? Why? Are you okay?"

"Because I'm not in love with him. And apparently, he's in love with me. Or was…whatever. But, yeah, I think I'm fine."

She looked confused. "Really?"

I nodded and finally glanced her way, my mind in a jumbled fog from the events of the night. "Yeah, really. You know…I think he swept me off my feet so much with his romance, and music, and…I just got lost in all of it. I was in love with being in love, I think. Because when he asked me if I loved him, I just *couldn't* say yes. And if you love someone, you should be able to say so, right?"

"I…guess," she answered slowly. "Are you sure you're okay?"

"I'm sure. It was actually the best breakup I've ever had. No fight, no cheatin', no drama. Just old-fashioned honesty. It was pretty refreshin'. He really *is* a nice guy. I hope we can be friends. He wasn't even mad or bitter toward me for not bein' in love with him. He handled it very maturely."

"Well, I guess I'm…happy for you then?"

I came out of my trance enough to glance at her and smile slightly. "Yes, be happy for me. I'm fine, Val. Seriously."

"Okay, well, can we go back to our table, then? We look kinda silly just standin' here in the middle of the dance floor, not movin'."

Oh, no. "Do you think everybody saw what happened? Are people talkin' about it?"

"No, not yet. It's too crowded for anybody to notice," she assured me. "But if we stand here much longer, they'll start to wonder what's up."

"All right, let's go sit down." We moved through the pulsing bodies until we cleared the dance floor. Of course, my friends asked where Rex was, so I gave them the short version. I said we'd broken up and he went home, but that I was fine and we ended on good terms. The rest of them were just as confused as Val had been. Rex and I must have seemed perfect together.

I sat for a while, not talking except to answer questions directed at me, and watched all the happy couples and friends having the time of their lives. I was lost in my own head when Kayla broke my train of thought.

"Now's your chance, Cora. I'm going out there to attempt to dance. Val convinced me, so you better come with us or you'll miss this humiliatin' experience," she joked.

I blinked and tried to focus, then stood and followed the girls. Dancing with them distracted me from my thoughts for a while and I actually started having a great time. They kept me dancing as long as possible, pretending it was Kayla who needed to be out there. I soon realized they were using her inability to dance as an excuse to keep me busy.

Val and I showed Kayla different moves and dances while the music pounded. After forty-five minutes of this, I was exhausted.

We headed back to our seats right as the DJ said it was time to announce prom king and queen.

I hadn't given the subject much consideration. It wasn't something a student campaigned for like homecoming court, which I'd successfully worked toward every year. Although I wasn't crowned homecoming queen this year, as I'd always hoped, it was an honor just to be on the court. So I hadn't thought much about prom queen until that very moment.

"Prom king and queen are great honors," the principal was saying in the DJ's microphone. "Since you all vote on your king and queen without the influence of campaigns, it's truly something to be cherished and appreciated."

"Blah, blah, blah…" Val mumbled.

Kayla and I laughed, but I secretly hoped to be queen. I knew it was unlikely since I hadn't been voted homecoming queen, and statistically, prom queens were also homecoming queens. I told myself not to get too hopeful. After all, it wasn't even something I'd thought about enough to actually *want* before tonight. Suddenly, though, I felt like being crowned would be a silver lining to my strange, not-so-perfect-after-all night.

"…and your prom king is…Landon Jester!"

My lips parted and my eyes widened as I watched Landon saunter up the red carpet onto the stage where he accepted his crown.

"Landon? I can't believe it," I muttered in shock.

His baseball buddies were cheering and hollering, and he pumped a fist in the air in victory. I was stunned. I didn't think he'd want this, but he seemed thrilled.

"…drum roll, please…Cora Stephens!" Principal Long called my name, but I wasn't sure I'd heard him right. I'd missed the first part of the sentence, so maybe I'd misheard the name.

"Cora! Oh, my gosh! You won, you're prom queen!" Val and Kayla both started talking at once, pushing me out of my chair.

"Wha—"

"Your prom queen is Cora Stephens! Miss Stephens, are you here?"

Whoa, I'd heard right. He was calling my name. I walked in a daze all the way to the podium. Everything and everyone was a blur. I couldn't focus on anything around me. I couldn't hear what was being said. All I heard was a steady buzzing sound. I don't know if I even leaned down when they crowned me. I was in a state of shock.

I finally came out of my daze and realized what was happening. A rush of excitement coursed through my body and I waved at my friends. As I scanned the crowd, I noticed that everyone was cheering. Until my eyes landed on Lacy...she stood with her arms crossed and her eyes narrowed, but I didn't care. Even *she* couldn't ruin my moment.

"And now it's time for our king and queen to share a special dance," I heard the DJ announce.

That's when I remembered I wasn't standing up there alone. Landon was right beside me, and we were expected to dance together—in front of everyone.

Oh, no, I thought. How would we handle this? My nerves became knots in my stomach as I slowly turned to evaluate his reaction. To my surprise, he had a soft smile on his face and his hand held out. The smile seemed so sincere that I couldn't help but return the gesture. I took his hand and we gazed into each other's eyes for a long moment.

The knots turned into butterflies and my knees suddenly felt like Jell-O. My heart was fluttering so quickly I thought it would jump right out of my chest. I wouldn't have been a bit surprised if everybody could hear how loudly it beat.

In that instant, as I stared into his caring eyes, every emotion I'd ever felt for him came rushing back. I saw each day spent together at his shed, each block party when he'd helped my father with the grill, each lazy-day trip to the store, each afternoon spent pushing one another on swings at the park, each breathtaking kiss, and each tear he'd wiped from my eyes. I felt friendship, security, happiness, passion, and...love. The last feeling was the strongest, and the most shocking.

I'd been kidding myself for months. Of course I was in love with Landon! He was right to have assumed I was afraid. I was scared of getting hurt or betrayed. I was scared to let myself be vulnerable again. Suddenly, the truth dawned on me. I thought dating Rex had been a way for me to get over Jeff and get on with my life, but in reality, I'd been using him to distract myself from the things I felt for Landon.

But right now, in this moment, none of that mattered. I loved him. I was madly, deeply in love with Landon.

This realization took all of one minute, even though it felt as if we stood frozen—gazing at each other—for hours. I floated on air as he led me to the center of the dance floor. I didn't even notice which song played as I snuggled close to him and swayed in rhythm with his body. I couldn't stop smiling.

"You're pretty excited about being prom queen, huh?" he asked.

I realized he misinterpreted the meaning behind my expression. "Yeah, I am. But that's not the only reason I'm happy."

Landon raised his eyebrows. "Really? What's the other reason? Did Rex do somethin' good?" His eyes narrowed—subconsciously, I was sure—when he said Rex's name.

"No... Actually, we broke up."

He paused for a split second, eyes wide, and then continued to sway. "I'm sorry to hear that."

I shrugged. "It's okay. We ended on good terms." I hesitated, pondering my next words, before announcing, "I wasn't in love with him."

Landon concealed a grin, but not before I noticed. "I see. And how'd he feel about that?"

"That's actually *why* we broke up. He said he loved me, but I couldn't say it back, so we went our separate ways."

Landon looked thoughtful. "So...you're happy because you two broke up?"

"No. I mean, yeah, I am...but that's not the reason I seem to have a hanger stuck in my mouth." I giggled, suddenly becoming nervous.

He laughed at my choice of words. "Well, what is it, Cora? The suspense is killin' me."

I bit my lip. I didn't want to just blurt out that I loved him. I wanted the moment to be special. "You'll have to wait 'til the end of the song. And then we'll go talk somewhere."

He rolled his eyes and chuckled. "You and your dramatics. All right, I'll be patient. But this better be good."

I grinned up at him. "Oh, it is."

We enjoyed the rest of the dance in silence. I leaned my head against his shoulder as he held me close. Sensations pulsed through my body—sensations I hadn't felt for him in a really long time.

He lifted my chin as the song ended and asked in a gruff voice, "You had somethin' to say?"

"Follow me," I replied mysteriously. I led him off the dance floor, past the circle of tables, and to a corner of the gym that was empty.

"Okay, we're far enough. Spit it out already!" He laughed.

I took a deep breath—suddenly I'd lost all my bravado. My hands shook as the butterflies returned to my stomach.

"Hey, you all right? What's goin' on?" Landon asked. Concern filled his eyes and worry creased his forehead.

I bit my lip and thought of how to begin. "Landon, we've been through a lot together and…" I hesitated. That didn't sound the way I'd intended.

"If this is about our conversation at your house a while back, you don't have to finish. I'm sorry about that. I didn't mean what I said. I've been miserable the past month and I want us to be friends again. I realized I'd rather have you as a friend than not have you at all. You're too important to me."

I took a deep breath. "Actually, that's what I wanted to talk to you about." I paused for effect. "It's too late…I don't wanna be your friend."

First disbelief, then anger flashed across his face. "What? Cora, you can't be serious. Did you really drag me over here just to tell me that? I can't believe this! You're really somethin' else. Somebody tries to tell you how they feel, and you can't handle it, so—"

"Landon!" I interrupted. "Please…you didn't let me finish."

"Oh. Sorry. Again." He exhaled. "I didn't mean to lose my temper like that, but you know me. I just—"

I had to shut him up again. But this time I decided to try a different approach. I put my hands on his cheeks and pulled his face down to mine. Then I crushed my lips against his just once, quickly.

"Whoa," he breathed when I released my hold.

I giggled, a little embarrassed. "What I was *tryin'* to say—before you so rudely interrupted—is that…I…love you." I paused, studying his reaction.

He just stood, unspeaking and motionless, for at least a full minute. Finally, he whispered, "Really? Are you sure?"

"Yeah, I'm sure. It's taken me a really, really long time to figure it out, but I *am* in love with you after all. I couldn't tell Rex I loved him because…well, because I love *you*. And I *just* realized it when you took my hand up there on that stage. And when you held me while we danced…" I trailed off, searching his eyes for a sign that he still felt something for me. When he didn't speak, I began to panic. "Am I too late?" I asked quietly. "That girl you're with…is she, I mean, are you two…together?"

He broke into a grin, grabbed me by the waist, and spun me around. "Are you kiddin'? Do you know how long I've waited to hear you say you love me?"

I laughed as he stopped spinning and put my feet back on the floor. I was still a little unsure about what would happen next. "But you didn't really answer my question about your date. I mean, you can't just ditch her…"

"She's not my date. She came with some guy she has a huge crush on. She was just dancin' with me to make him jealous because he was flirtin' with another girl," Landon explained.

"Oh, good," I replied with relief.

He chuckled for a second, and then his face turned serious. "Cora Stephens," he said, his voice and eyes soft, "I love you. Actually, love doesn't even describe the way I feel about you. It's too cliché. You…you're my heart and soul. My reason for livin'. I've loved you since the first time I saw you, when you had on that bright pink puffy dress in the third grade and you introduced yourself to me as 'Princess Cora.' And now here you are, in another pink dress, openin' up *your* heart and soul to *me*. And it feels more amazin' than I ever imagined."

My heart raced at his words. It thudded against my chest as he drew me into his arms. I reached up and touched his cheek, soaring in bliss. His head bent slightly and I responded by lifting my chin until our lips met again. This kiss was softer, magical. My head spun while the kiss grew more passionate. After a few minutes, he reluctantly pulled away.

"Well, now that all this is settled, what do ya say we enjoy the rest of our prom night?" he asked.

With that, we rejoined our friends. I got my perfect prom evening after all.

CHAPTER THIRTEEN

I awoke the next morning in a state of undeniable ecstasy. I called Landon as soon as I was dressed and asked him to come over. I couldn't wait to see him again.

When I heard Landon drive up, I met him at the door and led him over to the front porch swing. We sat on the swing, holding hands and talking. "So…I have a question," I said.

"Shoot," he replied.

"I've been thinking about that conversation we had in my bedroom, the one that kept us apart for a month. Anyway, you said somethin' about givin' me up to somebody else before. What'd you mean?"

"Ugh," he moaned. "Wish I hadn't said that."

"What, Landon?"

"Don't get mad, all right?"

I eyed him curiously. "Okay…"

He took a breath and exhaled it slowly. "When you and me were together a couple years ago, I overheard you tellin' Valerie you thought Jeff was cute. I let it go for a while, but then I heard rumors that he wanted to ask you out. The day before we broke up, I saw the two of you talkin'. You were smilin' and seemed real happy..." He paused, his eyes boring into mine. "I didn't wanna stand in the way of your happiness, Cora. So...I thought about it a lot and decided to let you go. It was the stupidest thing I've ever done and I regretted it every day."

"Wow," I breathed. "I had no idea. Why didn't you just talk to me?"

"Come on, Cora. I didn't stand a chance against a star football player. I felt like I wasn't good enough for you, that you deserved somebody better. But then he turned out to be a jerk, and I kicked myself for givin' you up so easy. I never would've done what he did, and I blamed myself for lettin' it happen. Ever since then, I've been the only guy I trust to keep you happy. That's why it was so hard for me to stand by and watch you with Rex. I didn't want you to get hurt again, and I knew in my heart that he wasn't right for you. Because *I'm* right for you. You and me...we're the real thing. I've always known it...I just wish I'd tried harder to make you see it."

I recalled our previous breakup and his saying we didn't have any chemistry. Everything finally made sense. He'd just said that so I wouldn't argue with his decision. He thought he was doing what was best for me. Because *of course* we had chemistry. How had I been so blind?

"Landon, do you know how many nights I spent awake tryin' to figure out what was goin' on with you and me? I mean, you have to understand where I was comin' from. You told me we were better off as friends, that we didn't have any chemistry. That's why I was confused when you said you loved me. *You* were the one that had ended our relationship. So I thought you were just bein' possessive with the whole Rex thing. I didn't realize..." I trailed off, staring at the ground. After a few seconds, I took a deep breath and continued. "But you were right about one thing, I *was* scared. I didn't want us to break up again, because then I'd lose you forever."

"Hey," he whispered, pulling my chin up until I met his gaze. "I'm sorry I put you through all that. If I'd just been honest with you about Jeff in the first place, none of it would've happened. And even if it had, at least you would've known exactly where you stood with me."

I shook my head. "It's not completely your fault. I was too stubborn to listen when you tried to tell me the truth. *I'm* the one who should be sorry. I'm sorry it took me so long to figure out my real feelings for you. And I'm sorry you had to stand by while I was with Jeff…and Rex."

"You know, we're pretty pathetic if you think about it." He chuckled.

"Hey! Speak for yourself," I retorted, slapping him playfully on the arm.

"No, it's a good pathetic. At least we're pathetic together."

I joined in his laughter. It felt so good to be with him. Just sitting next to him made my heart race. "Well, it's all behind us now. We only have our future to look forward to."

"You're right. And I promise I'll never hide the truth from you again, Cora. You'll always know exactly what I'm feelin'."

I reached over and kissed his cheek. "Same here."

A week later, rain splattered my windshield and sheeted down on the road in front of me as I drove to meet up with Val and Kayla. Trees bent and waved in the wind. A storm was definitely headed our way, putting a damper on my and my friends' plans to spend our Saturday at the park.

I pulled into a parking spot in front of the local coffee shop—where we had decided to meet due to the weather—and put the car in park. I cut the engine and grabbed a pink umbrella from under the passenger seat. Bracing myself, I put the umbrella in position and threw open my door. I released the umbrella and got out of my car simultaneously. The flip-flops I donned splashed water onto my bare ankles and calves as I hurried across the small parking lot.

Val and Kayla were already at a table—coffee and bagels in hand—when I entered. I closed my umbrella, propped it up beside the door, and shook water from my feet before joining them.

"Well, she finally made it!" Val joked as I pulled out a chair and plopped down.

"I'm sorry, y'all," I apologized. "I kept tryin' to leave, but Mama wouldn't stop askin' questions. 'Are you gonna see Landon today? Did you hear about his dad's promotion? When will he join us for dinner? What are you gonna do in the fall when you go to New York?'" I mimicked. "I swear, that woman's gonna drive me crazy!" I sighed, rolling my eyes. It had been exactly a week since prom and my declaration of love to Landon, and Mama was still buzzing about it. She'd always liked Landon, so there was no doubt in my mind that she was thrilled with the new development.

"What *are* you gonna do in the fall?" Kayla asked.

I averted my eyes, pondering the issue that had been bugging me for days. I would leave for fashion school in New York in just a few months, and Landon would be here. He was enrolled in the community college about twenty minutes from Davis. We hadn't mentioned the separation, but I knew he was just as worried as I was about it.

I looked at Kayla. "I honestly don't know. We haven't even talked about it."

"This really stinks," she complained. "You two *just* got together, and now you only have a little while before you're pushed apart again."

I nodded, drumming my manicured fingernails on the cool marble tabletop. Valerie put her hand over mine, constraining my fingers, and said, "I'm glad you finally admitted your feelings for him. I've always known y'all are perfect for each other. But it's gonna be really hard when you're so far away. It's somethin' you should talk to him about before it happens. You need to make a plan now. You know, set aside time to talk to each other every day, and decide how many times you'll fly down here and how many times he'll go there every month."

Kayla's eyes lit up at the mention of a plan. "Yeah, Val's right! All you need is a strategy. As long as you have a predetermined strategy, you'll be fine." Kayla was the most organized person I knew. Just the idea of a plan—or "strategy," as she called it—turned everything around. She honestly believed that with the right organization, anything could work.

I prayed a smile would hide the doubt weighing heavily on my shoulders. "Thanks, y'all, that's good advice. I'll talk to him about it soon," I said. Even though it won't make much of a difference, my subconscious mocked. Despite my friends' optimistic encouragement, deep down, I knew all the logic and planning in the world couldn't possibly suffice when it came to matters of the heart.

My chair scraped the hardwood floor as I stood. "I'll be right back. Gonna grab some coffee." I headed to the counter and placed my order. A few minutes later, I took my vanilla latte back to where the girls sat, but I remained standing.

"So, what do y'all wanna do?" I asked.

"We could go shoppin'," Kayla suggested.

"Yeah!" Valerie agreed enthusiastically. "I need some new shorts for summer."

"Sounds good," I replied. "Should we stay around here or go to the mall?"

Since Davis was such a small town, we didn't have our own mall. We had a couple of major department stores and a few mom-and-pop shops, but no mall. A neighboring city, Bensonville, boasted the closest mall, so that's where most citizens of Davis shopped when they craved more than what our town offered.

"Let's go to the mall," Val said in response to my question. "I think a day trip to Bensonville'll be fun!"

Although it only took about half an hour to get there, people— especially teenagers—made a big deal out of visiting Bensonville. I figured all the excitement was the result of small-town life.

Kayla and Valerie stood and grabbed their trash, then we headed for the door. They threw their trash away as I picked up my umbrella.

"We can take my car," I suggested. "I've got a full tank of gas." They agreed and we pushed open the coffee shop door, braced ourselves, and ran for my car.

Thirty minutes later, we pulled up to the mall and parked. It had stopped raining, but we carried our umbrellas anyway. Once we made it to the mall entrance, we sat down on a bench and each called our parents to let them know our whereabouts.

My mother was agitated when I informed her we were in Bensonville. "Cora, I didn't want you leavin' town today," she lectured. "There've been some things happenin' at that mall lately, so I want you to come home now."

I groaned internally. "But we just got here, Mama. And you didn't say anything this mornin' about not leavin' town. Besides, we always come here."

There was silence on the line, which meant she was either really mad or that she was contemplating my argument. Finally, she sighed in exasperation. "All right, Cora. Since I didn't *specifically* forbid this, I won't make you come home. But please, please be careful. And you girls stay together."

Yes!

"We will, Mama."

"Okay, bye, sweetie. Love you."

"Love you too," I replied before hitting the "end" button on my phone.

"Everything good?" Val inquired when she saw my expression.

"Yeah, just Mama bein' over-protective, as usual. She said she didn't want me comin' to this mall. But I talked her out of makin' me go home."

Kayla frowned. "That's weird. My dad said the same thing...somethin' about a high crime rate."

I observed our surroundings. Everything about this place radiated "safe family town," from the perfectly trimmed hedges to the newly renovated exterior of the mall. There was a carousel and fountain at the front entrance, both bordered by brightly colored flowers. Even with people sloshing through puddles and pushing their way to the doors, the site appeared peaceful.

"Ha," Val remarked. "This place is probably safer than Davis. I'm sure they can afford to pay their cops pretty well here. They've got security at practically every corner."

I glanced in the direction she pointed and noticed several security guards spaced evenly around different entrances. "Yeah," I agreed. "I feel pretty safe."

CHAPTER FOURTEEN

The muffled notes of country music woke me from a deep sleep on Sunday morning. I groaned and flipped onto my stomach, burying my head under the pillow. The girls and I had stayed at the mall until it closed, shopping and chatting. We'd decided to see a movie afterwards, so I didn't get home until close to midnight.

When the song didn't stop, I realized it was my cell phone. I sat up unsteadily, rubbed my eyes, and reached for the phone on my nightstand. Landon's name flashed across the screen. My heart thudded quickly and a grin spread across my face. I cleared my throat but still sounded groggy when I said hello.

"Hey, sleepy head," Landon crooned in a way that sent a feeling of warmth all the way down to my toes.

I glanced at the antique clock hanging on my wall. Six o'clock? "It is *way* too early, Landon!" I complained.

He chuckled. "Figured you'd say that, so I planned somethin' I think you'll like…to make up for it."

I smiled and hugged a pink and black striped pillow to my chest, sitting cross-legged on my bed. "Oh, really?" I asked, intrigued. "And just what'd you plan?"

"It's a surprise. Can you be ready in thirty minutes?" he asked, sounding as excited as a kid on Christmas morning.

His enthusiasm was contagious. "Thirty minutes? Landon, it's six in the mornin'! What in the world are we gonna do this early?"

He laughed. "Just trust me."

"Fine, but don't be mad if I stink. I don't think I can shower *and* be ready with such short notice."

I could hear the smile in his voice when he responded. "I won't get too close," he teased.

"Well, I didn't say *that*. I just said don't get mad."

"It's a deal. I'll be there to pick you up in half an hour. We're on a tight schedule, so be ready."

"Okay, bye!" Anticipation washed over me and sent chills down my arms as I jumped out of bed. I had absolutely no idea what he could possibly have in store for us, but I was glad just to spend the morning with him. The past week had been the happiest of my life, and I knew things could only go up from here.

I couldn't stop grinning as I washed my face, brushed my teeth, and threw on a pair of old jeans and a bright blue fitted tank top. I checked the clock on my phone, running a brush through my hair.

Five minutes.

I had just enough time to put on a little mascara, blush, and lip gloss. Once finished, I took a deep breath and appraised my appearance. Although it was an understated look, I felt pretty in a simple way. But then, I'd felt pretty every moment since prom. It was hard *not* to with Landon constantly complimenting me. My self-esteem had doubled in a matter of days.

Deana Carter's voice shrilled out the lyrics to *Strawberry Wine* at the exact moment I was slipping on a pair of white flip-flops. My phone—Landon's signal. I hit the ignore button and walked over to my window, pulling the ivory curtains aside to see his jeep in the driveway. My heart skipped a beat when I saw him. I couldn't make out what he was wearing since the sun still wasn't up, but I knew he'd be handsome in anything. He was looking in my direction, so I gave him a wave to let him know I was on my way down.

I grabbed my purse and gave myself one last glance in the mirror, just to check. I opened my bedroom door slowly and crept down the hallway to the stairs. I tip-toed down the steps to avoid any creaking that might wake my parents. Once downstairs, I rushed through the living room and unlocked the door as quietly as possible. Then I paused for a split second, deciding I should leave a note for Mama.

Grabbing a scrap piece of paper and pen from a drawer in the dining room, I jotted, *With Landon. Should be back in time for church.*

I then stuck the note under a magnet on the refrigerator and backtracked through the kitchen and dining room to the living room, and finally made it outside. Landon got out of his jeep and met me halfway. He threw his arms around my waist and spun me around. "I missed you yesterday," he whispered in my ear after we stopped spinning.

I smiled and bit my lip. "I missed you too."

Then he took my hand and led me to the jeep, opening the door and helping me in. "You look beautiful."

Blood warmed my cheeks as I looked into his piercing blue eyes. "Even though I haven't had a shower?" I kidded.

He shook his head with a grin. "I never would've known. And for the record…you smell wonderful." Then he winked at me and I melted.

"Thank you, Landon." My pulse raced as he brushed his hand gently across my cheek. It raced even faster as he slowly leaned toward me, our faces inching closer with each passing second until our lips finally met. The kiss was soft and slow and sent warmth through my entire body.

He finally pulled away. "We better get goin'," he said in a husky voice. Then he closed my door and walked around to get in the driver's seat. We rode in comfortable silence for a few minutes. He drove down some dirt roads that I wasn't familiar with for a while. The scenery reminded me of finding Jeff and Lacy together, and I was amazed at how much had changed since that horrible day.

A few minutes later, Landon pulled over and turned to me. "Here, put this on," he instructed, getting a scarf from the back seat.

I tilted my head in confusion. "You want me to wear a scarf? I *did* brush my hair, but if you think it looks that bad…"

Landon chuckled. "No, it's a blindfold. Turn around, I'll help you."

I did as I was told and he tied the scarf gently around my eyes. Once Landon was sure the fabric securely blocked my vision, I leaned back against the seat. "So are you gonna tell me why I'm wearin' a blindfold?" I inquired.

"Because all this is a surprise, and I don't want you seein' where we're goin'. You might figure it out."

"Oh, okay. Gotcha," I said with a grin. I couldn't hide my excitement any more than he could hide his. I loved surprises, and I had a feeling this was going to be a pretty good one.

Landon pulled back onto the road and began to drive once more. A short while later, we came to a stop. "Can I take this thing off now?" I asked impatiently.

"Nope, not yet," he answered.

He opened his door, hopped out of the jeep, and came around to help me. The ground crunched under our feet as he led me through what I imagined to be a wooded area. The air smelled fresh, and the sound of crickets chirping reminded me that it was still early.

We finally stopped walking and Landon untied my blindfold. "All right, are you ready?" he asked before letting the blindfold drop.

"I'm ready, I'm ready!" I exclaimed, bouncing from foot to foot. He pulled the blindfold off my face, and I gasped. It was the most beautiful view I'd ever seen—just like a painting. The woods opened up to reveal the spot we'd nicknamed "Magnolia Lake" as children. The lake—which was actually just a pond—was partially shaded by a huge, beautiful Southern Magnolia tree in full bloom. The previous day's storm had blown several blooms off the tree, decorating the water with floating white flowers.

Beginning where we stood, several miniature lanterns were placed carefully on the ground and formed a path to a blanket laid out by the water's edge. As the sun rose, it created a picturesque backdrop of pink hues in the sky.

I noticed two plates and goblets, along with a few crystal dishes, arranged on the blanket. "Wow, Landon," I breathed, mesmerized. "This is amazing."

"You really like it?" he asked.

"Of course I do! It's beautiful!"

"It's nothin' compared to you," he said softly.

I blushed and squeezed his hand. "So what's all that on the blanket?"

"Breakfast," he replied with a grin. "Come on, are you hungry?"

I shrugged, smiling. "I could eat."

"Good." He pulled me after him down the lantern-lined pathway, and then we sat on the blanket.

"This is crazy!" I laughed. "What's in all these dishes?" He sat down, uncovering one dish at a time. There were huge blueberry muffins, strawberries, peaches, brownies, bagels, and orange juice. I stared wide-eyed at the spread. "Did you make all this?" I asked incredulously.

"Yeah," he said. "Well, Mom gave me the recipes and some instructions, since I've never baked before. But, yeah, I made all of it. I mean, really just the muffins and brownies."

I kissed his cheek. "It's wonderful, Landon. I can't believe you went to so much trouble for me. You must've been up at three o'clock this mornin'."

"You're worth it, Cora," he replied. "Besides, it was nothin'. Just thought it'd be cool to eat breakfast and watch the sun come up together. The view's awesome from here."

I sighed contentedly, taking in the scene before me. "I can't believe you remembered this spot."

"That month we weren't talkin' I came here all the time to think. I'd sit here and listen to the birds, and just think. I vowed to bring you here if we ever worked stuff out."

"Well, I sure am glad we did."

"Me too," he said. "Now let's eat!"

We ate quietly for a few minutes, enjoying the sounds of nature. He moved to sit behind me as the sun started to rise, wrapping his arms around my stomach. I leaned my head back on his chest and nestled in closer to him.

The sky was a beautiful shade of pink while the sun rose to reveal all its glory. As sunlight reflected on the ripples of Magnolia Lake, I said a silent prayer of awe. It was in moments like these that I could truly feel the beauty and grace of God. Even though I'd grown up in a Christian home and had been to church nearly every Sunday of my life, my faith often got pushed out of mind through the everyday routine and struggles of life. But then, to witness a sunrise as beautiful as this made me wonder how anyone could *not* believe in God.

"You ready to go?" Landon's voice interrupted my serene thoughts an hour later.

I closed my eyes and sighed happily. "Sure. I could stay out here all day, though."

"Me too," he said. "But we should get back. I'm supposed to help my parents with some yard work this morning before church. Then we can spend the rest of the day together."

I smiled up at him, amazed at what a wonderful son he was. Wonderful son, wonderful boyfriend, wonderful person. I sent up another silent prayer, thanking God for giving me this time with such a special guy. I knew it was too soon—and I was too young— to think about marriage, but I could easily see myself married to Landon. Together forever.

"In that case, take me home now, mister!" I teased.

He stood and pulled me up so that we were face to face. We embraced and he pressed his mouth to mine again, this time with more passion and strength. Then we made our way back home. Landon dropped me off with a smile and a hug, promising to come over after church.

Mama was waiting for me when I walked into our house, expecting a full report of my previous whereabouts. When I told her what my amazing boyfriend had done, she was speechless.

"Isn't that the most romantic thing you've ever heard?" I asked, still in my dream-like state.

Mama blinked. "It sure is," she replied. "I can't believe a high school boy could come up with something so…grown-up."

"I'm a lucky girl. I'm gonna go get ready now." I kissed her cheek and headed toward the stairs, bounced up them, and skipped into my bedroom. Nothing could steal my happiness.

CHAPTER FIFTEEN

"What's that?" Val asked Monday morning as I pulled a note out of my locker.

I shrugged. "Don't know," I responded, ripping open the square, white envelope and tugging a piece of stationary out of it.

You're the most beautiful and sweet girl I've ever met. Be mine.

Your Secret Admirer.

The words were typed, I assumed for the purpose of remaining anonymous.

"Oooo, a secret admirer!" Val exclaimed, reading over my shoulder. "Wonder who it is? This is excitin'!"

I smiled and hugged my schoolbooks to my chest. "It's from Landon, Val," I answered with a thudding heart. "He's *so* sweet. Yesterday mornin', he surprised me with breakfast by Magnolia Lake...at sunrise." I continued the story, not leaving out a single detail.

She listened, wide-eyed, until I finished describing the beautiful sunrise and delicious food. "Wow," she said. "He's a closet romantic! Who knew?"

I laughed. "Yeah. He was always sweet when we were together before, and every once in a while he'd bring me flowers or something, but this was so beyond anything any guy has *ever* done for me!"

She grinned, but then her face turned serious as if she were pondering something. "Hmmm…"

"What?"

She glanced from me, to the note I held, then back to me. "Well…not to burst your bubble or anything, but why would Landon send you a secret admirer note? Why wouldn't he just sign his name to it? He knows that you know he loves you. So why the secret part?"

I shook my head, shrugging. "I don't know. Maybe he thinks it's more romantic this way. Maybe he's just bein' creative."

With raised eyebrows, she answered, "Maybe."

I stuffed the note back in its envelope and put it in my purse. Shutting my locker door, I turned back to Val and said, "It's gotta be Landon. Who else would send me a love note?" Then we walked together to class.

Each day for the next two weeks, there was a new secret admirer note in my locker. I never mentioned them to Landon because I didn't want to spoil his fun. If he had some surprise these notes were leading to, I didn't want to ruin it.

On Friday of the second week, the final note read:

It's been long enough. Meet me at the back of the student parking lot this afternoon. I'll be the one with a red rose.

I told Val and Kayla about the last note while we primped in the restroom during our lunch period that day. I could hardly contain my excitement. "I can't wait to see what Landon's been up to!" I said, concluding the story. "This is gonna be so good!"

"And he hasn't dropped a single hint?" Kayla asked.

"Nope, he's been completely secretive about it," I replied with a smile.

"What'd all the other notes say? Did they give away any ideas about what's goin' on?" Val chimed in.

"Mm-mm," I answered, running a brush through my hair in front of the restroom mirror. "They all just said sweet things about my skin, my eyes…ya know, stuff like that. A different compliment each time."

Val eyed me curiously. "And what happens if the guy waitin' for you isn't Landon?"

Kayla met Val's gaze. "You don't think it's Landon?" she asked.

"I mean, it's possible. I just don't understand why he wouldn't sign the notes from him instead of a secret admirer. After all, it's no *secret* he admires Cora."

"Y'all," I interrupted. "It's Landon. It has to be. One of the notes said somethin' about the birthmark on the back of my neck. Nobody else would know about that. It's usually covered by my hair."

I saw my friends exchange an odd look. "What?"

"*Jeff* would know about that birthmark," Kayla said hesitantly.

Val's eyes grew big, and she looked as if she'd just pieced together a puzzle. "Of course he'd know about it! And didn't he tell you he still loved you a while back? *Now* this makes sense."

My forehead creased and my eyes narrowed in thought. "No way," I said after a moment. "I made it very clear to him that we have no future. That I've moved on."

Kayla pursed her lips. "Just don't be upset if it's not Landon in the parkin' lot today, okay?"

"It'll *be* him," I answered stubbornly as we made our way out of the restroom and back to the table to join our friends.

Later that afternoon, my heart hammered as I pushed through the doors of Davis High. I was headed to the student lot to see what Landon had planned for us. I was so wound up that I had to force myself to walk at a normal pace rather than run to meet him as fast as humanly possible.

A few long minutes later, I skidded to an abrupt stop. My breath came out in one swift gush. I blinked.

The person standing in front of me holding a red rose—as promised—was *not* Landon.

"Jeff?" I whispered unbelievingly, eyes wide and mouth gaping open.

He took a few steps toward me, extending the rose. "Hey, baby. I guess you got my notes."

I shook my head, still wide-eyed with shock. "Jeff, what the—"

He grabbed my hand before I could finish the question, placing the stem of the rose in my palm and closing my fingers around it. "I'm still in love with you. I never stopped lovin' you. I want you back."

I sighed in exasperation. "Jeff, we've already been through this. We're not gettin' back together. I've moved *on*."

His eyes narrowed and he clenched his jaw. "So…what? Now you're back with Landon? You'd rather be with *him* than me? He's a loser, Cora."

"He's twice the man you'll *ever* be," I hissed through clenched teeth. How dare he drop this bomb on me and then insult Landon! After everything he'd already put me through in the last year!

He huffed, "Right. I could take him."

I rolled my eyes, restraining myself from slapping Jeff across the face. "Nobody's gonna *take* anybody, okay? I'm not havin' this conversation with you again. We. Have. No. Future." I said the last sentence slowly, emphasizing each word.

He glared at me with such fury that fear pulsed through my veins. "I get it. You're too good for me now, right? You can just go from guy to guy, so you don't need me anymore," he growled. "First it was that kid livin' across the street from you, then you got bored with him and went after your *precious* Landon again. You ain't the girl I knew. You turned into a tease."

I winced, taking a small involuntary step back. Jeff inched closer. "Don't just stand there lookin' shocked," he said. "Tell me I'm wrong."

When I didn't respond, he continued the insults. "You can't tell me that, can you? I bet you gave yourself to both those guys. You acted so innocent with me, always tryin' to save yourself for marriage. Leadin' me on and teasin' me. Now look at you."

Rage boiled inside me and I finally lost it. "You don't know *anything* about me, Jeffrey! And you sure as heck don't know anything about Rex or Landon. They're decent guys, unlike you. Neither one of them ever tried to pressure me into somethin' I wasn't ready for, like you *always* did. You're a liar and a creep, and I'm sorry I was so nice to you last time. I should've told you then to shove off. But I didn't, so I'm tellin' you now." I paused, taking a breath to calm myself. Then, in a tight voice, I said, "Don't *ever* try to talk to me again. Because if you do, I swear on my life I'll call the police. This is harassment and I won't put up with it."

With that, I spun away from him so quickly that I almost lost my balance. I began to storm off, but Jeff's sudden grip on my arm stopped me. "I'm not scared of you, Cora," he said through clenched teeth, his hold getting tighter by the second. "This ain't over. Not even close."

I shuddered at his words, preparing myself to scream so that he'd let go of me. But before I had a chance to open my mouth, he dropped my arm and brushed past me. I sighed in relief and collapsed on the ground in one motion. I'd never felt physically threatened by Jeff before. Even though he'd sometimes emotionally intimidated me, I never thought he'd go this far. My head spun as I replayed the conversation.

Once the fear and shock finally subsided, I felt confused. The last time we'd spoken, he'd seemed so sincere and remorseful. Like a person who'd lost someone he loved. But this time…this time he was completely different. A person I'd never known before, not the same guy I'd dated for two years. Not the guy I had loved and cherished. No, the Jeff from today was not the same Jeff with whom I'd once been overwhelmingly infatuated.

With these disturbing thoughts in my head, I slowly pulled myself up off the ground and walked, trance-like, back to my car.

The next day, Landon and I were sitting together on my porch swing when he noticed the bruise on my arm. "What happened here?" he asked, gently touching the spot in question.

I'd avoided telling him about the encounter with Jeff because I knew he would get upset and worry about me. I bit my bottom lip. There was no use in lying. *Might as well go ahead and get it over with.* "Actually…Jeff did that. He grabbed my arm yesterday afternoon while we were talkin'."

Landon's eyes narrowed immediately and his hands curled into fists. "What? He grabbed you hard enough to leave a mark? Why didn't you tell me right away? I would've—"

"I know what you would've done," I said, cutting him off. "That's why I didn't tell you. It wouldn't have solved anything. Plus, I didn't think the bruise would still be there today."

His face became soft when he noticed my embarrassment. "I guess you're right. I probably would've got myself expelled or somethin' for fightin' that jerk."

"Exactly. I didn't wanna worry you for no reason."

He frowned. "Cora, he put a bruise on you. That's a good reason to worry. What were y'all talkin' about anyway?"

I hesitated, unsure if I should tell Landon the details of mine and Jeff's conversation. It'd only make him want to fight Jeff even more. Then again, I felt the sudden need to confide in Landon and tell him the whole messy thing, starting with the secret admirer notes. So I did.

"He threatened you?" Landon growled. "Where's that creep live? I'll teach him to mess with you." He stood, pacing back and forth on the porch. Finally, he sat down on the top step and leaned against the railing. "We have to do somethin' about this," he announced after a minute of pondering.

I stood and went to sit by him on the step. Putting my head on his shoulder, I asked, "But what can we do? He didn't actually make a threat against my life or anything. All he said was that it's not over. As far as the police are concerned, that could just mean more notes."

Landon sighed and put his arm around my waist. "I know you're right, but we can't just let him get away with it. Maybe I should have a little chat with him."

Abruptly, I picked up my head and looked at him in horror. "No, Landon! I don't want you gettin' involved, not like that. Anything could happen."

"I'm not scared of him."

"I know, and I'm not sayin' you'd lose a fight to him. But...you didn't see his expression. It was pure rage. There's no tellin' what he'd do."

Landon searched my face. "If you think it's that serious then we *have* to go to the cops...before he does somethin' crazy."

Shaking my head, I hugged his waist. "No, I don't think that's necessary. I'm probably just overreactin'."

He sighed as if realizing he'd lost and that he'd never convince me to call the police. "Okay, but I'll be keepin' an eye on him...*and* you. The more time you spend with me, the better."

"Now *that* I can live with," I answered with a grin.

CHAPTER SIXTEEN

The time flew by so quickly that I couldn't understand how graduation was only a day away. Final exams had come and gone, yearbooks had been signed, and the senior class had enjoyed one last rendezvous—a day at the city park, playing Frisbee and cherishing our last bit of time together as seniors.

Now it was Friday, and graduation would be the next evening at seven o'clock on the football field of Davis High. But first would be the Baccalaureate ceremony…which would begin at the Second Baptist Church of Davis in exactly eight hours.

For this reason, I was panicked.

In all the hustle and bustle of end-of-school-year activities and get-togethers, not to mention finals, I'd completely forgotten to get a dress for the night's event. The graduation dress was no problem. I'd purchased it months ago. However, I still needed something elegant—yet not too fancy—to wear for Baccalaureate.

I picked up the antique Victorian-style telephone in my bedroom and dialed Val's home number. Her mom answered and said that she was out, so I tried her cell. When I still couldn't reach her, I gave up and decided to call Kayla.

"Hey, Cora!" Kayla answered in her typically cheerful voice.

"Hey, Kayla. What're you up to?" I asked. I hoped she'd be free because I was in desperate need of a shopping buddy, someone to help me make a decision on the perfect dress for the evening.

"Nothin' really," she stated. "Just bein' lazy today until Baccalaureate. What's goin' on with you?"

I twisted the cool, plastic phone cord around my finger. "Well, don't laugh at me," I began, "but I need a dress for tonight." I heard a gasp on the other end of the line.

"You seriously don't have a dress for tonight yet?" Kayla asked in shock.

"No…I kinda forgot about it until this morning. I mean, I have my graduation dress, but I need somethin' to wear to tonight's ceremony. Isn't it supposed to be white?"

"Yeah. So did you wanna borrow somethin'? I'm not sure if I have another white dress…" Kayla trailed off, obviously concerned about my situation.

"Oh, no." I replied. "No, don't worry about that. I was just hopin' you could go shoppin' with me."

"Sure, of course! What time do ya wanna go?"

I glanced at my wall clock. "Um…now, if possible?"

Twenty minutes later, I heard a car door shut and pushed aside the curtains in my bedroom. Kayla was out of her car and headed to the front door. I grabbed my purse, took a quick glance in the mirror, and skipped down the steps just as a knock sounded on the door.

I nearly knocked Mama over as I hurried to greet Kayla. "Where are you goin' in such a rush?" she asked.

"I have to get a dress for tonight, so we're goin' to the mall," I explained, holding my breath in hopes that she wouldn't try to forbid me from going like the last time. I let that breath out when Mama just nodded and told us to be careful.

"See ya in a little while. Love you, Mama!"

A couple of hours and a million dresses later, I was exasperated. "I can't believe there's not a single decent white dress in this *entire* place!" I complained as Kayla and I walked around what seemed like the hundredth store we'd visited.

"Don't worry, we'll find somethin'." Kayla was the eternal optimist.

My fingers brushed lightly over the various materials of clothes hanging from a nearby rack and I groaned in frustration. "We've almost been through the whole mall, and we have exactly thirty minutes left before we need to go home. I don't know what I'm gonna do."

Suddenly, Kayla's eyes grew wide and she shook her head with a grin.

"What is it, Kay?" I asked.

"We forgot about the new store! I think it's called Serendipity…" She trailed off, frowning. "Now, if only I could remember where it is."

"Oh, my gosh, you're a life-saver!" I squealed. "I went in there once a while back, and they have tons of cute dresses! I think it's on the bottom floor, close to Victoria's Secret. Let's go!" With renewed excitement, we practically ran down the escalator to the new store. I gasped as we entered what could only be described as a girl's ultimate dream. The place was full of gorgeous dresses, fabulous shoes, and stunning jewelry. They'd also redecorated since the last time I'd been there. Everything was soft pink and black, with a Paris theme. The lights were dim, and soft Parisian music played in the background. This seemed like a good omen, since the style was similar to my bedroom decor.

"Wow," Kayla breathed.

"I know." Once we'd finally shaken ourselves back to reality, we split up to look for white dresses. In fifteen minutes, we met at the dressing rooms, each holding three items. I tried them all on, one by one, and began to get discouraged again when none of them fit or seemed good enough for the occasion…until I tried on the last one. It was knee-length, fitted, and strapless. Just above the waistline was a slim faux-pearl band, with a subtle off-white rose nestled on the right side. It was elegant and beautiful.

"It's gorgeous!" Kayla gushed when I stepped out of my dressing room modeling the fabulous creation. "You look absolutely amazing! Do you like it?"

I grinned at her and nodded my head. "This is the one!"

We took the dress over to the sales clerk to check out. After I'd paid and the clerk had wrapped up the dress, Kayla and I decided to stop in the food court to get fruit smoothies for the ride home. As we walked out of the mall, we chatted about graduation.

"I can't believe we graduate tomorrow," Kayla said. "It feels like yesterday we were scared freshmen just tryin' to blend in."

"Mmm-hmm," I mumbled distractedly. I could have sworn I'd heard footsteps behind us. I stopped for a second and turned around. There was no one in view. Shaking off the weird feeling, I tried to concentrate on what Kayla was saying.

"Do you remember sophomore year, when we skipped fifth period to get tickets for that Kenny Chesney concert?" she asked.

Laughing, I nodded my head. "Yeah, I can't believe we convinced you to skip!" I joked. She was a star student—never missed school and made straight As. While Valerie and I had spent most of our spare time over the last four years cheerleading and becoming social princesses, Kayla had spent hers focused on becoming Valedictorian. It was a goal she'd accomplished with ease. Even though I would graduate with honors the next day, I'd never put as much effort into my education as Kayla. I admired her dedication. "By the way," I inquired, "have you finished your Valedictorian speech yet?"

"Yeah, last week. I'm so nervous, though! Gettin' up and speakin' in front of the whole school...that's definitely more your territory than mine." She sighed. "Maybe you could give the speech on my behalf?"

"No way!" I said, nudging her. "You've worked for this your whole life. Get up there and enjoy your moment of fame! It's such a huge accomplishment. Be proud of it and let that pride show through your speech tomorrow. And in case I haven't told you, I think it's awesome that you're our Valedictorian. I really admire you for it."

She smiled sheepishly. "Thanks, Cora."

"You're welcome," I replied before taking a sip of my smoothie, which wasn't very good. We'd just made it to her car when I spotted a trashcan a few rows over. "I'll be right back," I said. "My smoothie's not any good. I'm gonna go throw it away in that trashcan over there. Will you put my stuff in the car?"

"Sure," she said, following my gaze. "I'll get the air goin' in here." I handed her my shopping bag and purse, then turned around as she got in the driver's seat and started her car.

As I backtracked through the parked vehicles, I heard footsteps again. Pausing, I looked around. Nobody was there. In fact, the entire parking lot seemed to lack a normal level of activity. There were plenty of cars, but there was not a single person walking around.

I shook my head to clear it, and started walking again—a little faster this time. Suddenly, I heard the sound again. Before I could turn around, something jabbed my back and a hand was over my mouth. I gasped and my whole body shook with fear. The smoothie I held slipped through my hand, splattering all over my shoes and jeans.

Suddenly, hot air blew in my ear at the same time I heard a deep voice say, "Don't make a sound or I'll push this knife through your back all the way into your heart." The gloved hand tightened over my mouth. "Now walk," the voice ordered.

My legs didn't move. I was completely frozen with terror. My mind raced as I contemplated what to do next. I knew Kayla couldn't see me. She was facing the opposite direction and there were too many cars between us. If I screamed I'd get stabbed, but it might give me a chance to wriggle free of this man's hold. I vaguely recalled a special on TV that said most attackers would back off if you screamed, no matter what they said. I tried to open my mouth, but the assailant's hold strengthened so that I couldn't even part my lips. My heart rate accelerated and I couldn't breathe. I was having a panic attack.

"I said move!" The stranger pushed me so hard I almost lost my balance, but then my legs finally seemed to work. I walked as he directed. We went straight for a minute, then he turned me to the right. After what felt like a thousand years, we were standing in front of a white, windowless work van. It was parked between a big jacked-up truck and a huge SUV. Nobody could see what was going on, if there was even anyone *in* the parking lot.

The side door opened and I stared into the face of another stranger. At least, I assumed he was a stranger. He wore a ski mask to hide his identity.

The first man shoved me into the van. There were no seats aside from the two in the front, so I fell backward and hit my head on something metal. I cringed and lay frozen for a minute. Then I saw what might be my only chance.

The first man stood in front of me, laughing. The second man leaned against the opposite side of the van, sitting cross-legged and messing with a cell phone.

I took a deep breath and kicked with all my strength, barely missing my attacker's groin. He doubled over and I scrambled to my hands and knees. My heart raced as I struggled to get out of the van. Just as I had one foot out, the second man grabbed my other foot, dragging me back.

Since I'd been half standing, the force of his pull caused me to thud against the van floor again, this time on my stomach. Then he grabbed my waist and flung me against the van wall next to him.

Tears sprung to my eyes as the first attacker, also wearing a ski mask, climbed into the van and slammed the door. I could only see his eyes, and they were staring at me with nothing but pure evil. Then I saw him lift something round—a paperweight maybe? I couldn't tell exactly what the object was, but I tried to back away as I realized what he intended to do with it. I closed my eyes, praying the blow would be quick.

CHAPTER SEVENTEEN

The next thing I knew, I heard strange voices discussing my situation. "I told you to bring her to me unharmed," the first one growled.

"She tried to escape. Kicked me in the gut!" the second guy argued.

"Yeah, man, we had no choice. She woulda got away. You wanted her here, we got her here. Now pay up." The three voices were muffled, and for a minute I thought they were the product of a crazy dream. Then I opened my eyes.

Fear immediately swept over me as I felt rope around my wrists and ankles. I was on my back, lying on a dirt floor. My hands were extended over my head, tied by the rope to a post that extended from the floor to the ceiling, which was comprised of wooden beams. As I studied my surroundings, I noticed the large room was divided into several smaller rooms. Stalls, maybe? The place was so run-down that it was hard to picture what it once could have been, but the longer I observed the details, the more convinced I became that I was being held in an old barn.

There was nobody else in the barn. Confusion creased my forehead. Maybe I *had* dreamt the voices.

Just then, a door behind me swung open. I whipped my head around to see who it was but quickly regretted that move. The left side of my head pounded so much that tears slid down my cheeks. I attempted to sit, but there was no way I could physically maneuver with my hands and ankles tied. Frustrated and scared, I began to sob.

"Come on, baby, don't cry. Here, let me help you up."

I sucked in a deep breath and tried to look toward the voice. It was oddly familiar, although I hadn't completely heard it through the sobs. I couldn't see its source, though, because the mystery guy squatted behind me and untied my arms, pulling me into a sitting position while he did it. Then he turned me to face him.

Oh, thank God! I started sobbing all over again, but this time I cried tears of relief. The face in front of me belonged to Jeff. I was safe.

He untied my legs, then pulled me close to him and stroked my hair. "Shh, it's okay. It's all gonna be okay. You won't be hurt anymore. I'm here now."

I calmed down long enough to try to make sense of the whole situation. Looking up at him, I asked, "What are you doin' here? How'd you find me?"

"I had a couple friends bring you to me. They weren't supposed to hurt you…I'm sorry 'bout that."

My heart dropped. "What?" Suddenly I was having trouble breathing again. Dread pulsed through my veins as I recalled Jeff's last words to me.

This ain't over, Cora. Not even close.

Shaking my head viciously, I attempted to scramble out of his hold, but his grip was suddenly restricting my body like a snake would its prey. *Oh, no…God help me!*

"Relax, baby," he said calmly. "I ain't gonna hurt you. I just wanted us to spend some time together and you weren't gonna let that happen. I didn't want it to be like this, but you didn't give me a choice."

I stopped struggling long enough to give him a look of utter disbelief. He was making this whole thing *my* fault? "You…had me *kidnapped*!" I whispered incredulously.

His face suddenly became tense and his eyes narrowed. "I *told* you. I didn't have any other choice."

Swallowing my fear, I decided to try and talk my way out of the danger into which I'd been thrust. If he was truly still in love with me—in some demented way—then I could use that to my advantage.

I took a shaky breath and began slowly. "But you *did* have a choice, Jeff," I said. "You could've left me alone. You could've *not* had those guys follow me and drag me here. What happened? I thought you loved me…isn't that what you said? That you never cared about Lacy, and that you wanted me back?" I paused, but when he didn't respond, I continued to reason with him in my most persuasive voice. "What we had was special. I know that. I was crazy about you…and maybe…maybe I *could* trust you again if you'd just let me go. Let me *choose* to love you. Don't force me." I bit my lip, praying my plan would work, knowing it was my only shot. He had to buy what I was selling. He just had to. I strongly sensed that my life depended on it.

Seconds ticked by. He seemed to be contemplating what I'd said, weighing the pros and cons…so I waited.

Another minute passed, and anxiety was beginning to get the best of me. Breathing gradually became more and more difficult, but I tried my best to hide it from Jeff. He needed to believe I'd really consider getting back together with him. If that's what he really wanted, then surely he'd agree to let me go. Then all I'd have to do was convince him I still loved him, get home, and call the police.

As these thoughts turned over in my head and I plotted my escape, Jeff continued to sit in the same spot, still gripping my arms.

Suddenly, he yanked me toward him with a hundred pounds of force, and before I realized what was happening, his lips crushed mine.

I froze. My mind screamed, "Kiss him back! Kiss him back!" But my body wouldn't cooperate. Terror had its claws around my heart so tightly that I couldn't force my lips to move. This was not the kind of kiss I remembered sharing with him. This kiss was forceful and harsh—painful. Teeth scraped against my bottom lip. Reflexively, I swung my head to the side.

Mistake.

I was on my back in an instant, and my head slammed against the floor. "I knew it!" he growled, holding my wrists over my head with one hand while he reached for the rope with his other. "You don't love me. All that stuff you just said was a lie. You didn't mean a single word. You were tryin' to trick me. Well, Cora baby, I'm done with it. You're gonna lay here 'til I get what I want."

"No, Jeff! Please let me go!" I cried. I struggled against him as he fought to get my wrists tied again the way they were before. But he was too strong for me.

Don't give up.

I screamed, not knowing if anyone would even hear my cries. Then, with as much force as I could possibly muster, I jerked an arm free and slapped the side of his head. He halted for a split second, and then his arm swung toward my face with a clenched fist.

And everything went black.

CHAPTER EIGHTEEN

There was no way to tell how long I'd been out once I regained consciousness. I was alone again, lying on my back with my ankles and wrists tied once more. There were no windows, and it was completely dark except for a dim lamp on the opposite side of the cold room.

Chills swept over me and I shivered uncontrollably. Glancing down, I realized the reason for that. I had been stripped of my shirt. My other clothes hadn't been removed, and I noticed my shirt lying on the floor just out of my reach.

Wondering if Jeff had simply taken my shirt to humiliate me, I began to sob hysterically. Memories of the previous day—or maybe the same day, since I had no perception of time—flooded my brain, right up to the punch that had rendered me unconscious.

Unending tears poured out of my eyes, and sobs turned my breaths into gasps. My entire body shook until I thought I might die of convulsions as I realized what was happening.

Jeff was holding me hostage.

After an eternity of hysterics, I became numb. I could no longer feel the hard ground against my back, or the tenderness in my face and head. I felt nothing. My eyes slid closed and I succumbed to the darkness and exhaustion.

When I finally awoke, I was propped up against the wall with a tray of food next to me on the floor, my wrists free from the rope that had previously restrained them. Instead, my legs were straight out in front of me, and my ankles now bound me to that dreadful wooden post with a chain lock. Still topless, I searched the area for my shirt. No such luck. I realized, to my dismay, that he did want to humiliate me—show me he was in charge.

A gurgling sound escaped my stomach, and I thought about food for the first time since I'd been taken from the mall. I was famished. I wondered silently how long it had been since I'd eaten. My glance drifted to the tray of food. My stomach rumbled again, but I didn't want to eat anything Jeff had touched. Not that he had put much effort into the meal. On the tray sat a bowl of tomato soup—normally my favorite—and a plate of saltine crackers. Out of curiosity I stuck my finger in the soup. *Ice cold.* Then I broke a cracker in half. *Stale.*

Stubbornness overcame me and I mentally refused to eat the food he'd so half-heartedly prepared. Maybe the soup had been warm when he brought it in. Still, it wasn't hard to make, just stick it in the microwave. Besides that, crackers don't go stale in a few hours. These were obviously old.

As I sat fuming and hungry, I heard a noise outside. I could barely make out the crunch of gravel under shoes. Then the doorknob wiggled until the door finally swung open. My heart raced, and I kept my eyes straight ahead rather than turning to watch Jeff enter.

Before I could count to ten, he was in front of me, looking down at the food with crossed arms. He squatted until his face was inches from mine. "Ya know, Cora, you could at least be grateful enough to eat the soup. I went to the trouble of bringin' it to you and you ain't even touched it."

Ignoring his remark, I jerked my head away from him and stared at the wall on the other side of the barn.

He let out a chuckle. "You always had a stubborn streak in you," he said, stroking my cheek. "It's one of the reasons I fell in love with you." He paused and dropped his hand, muttering, "But now it's just rude. Eat!"

I jumped involuntarily when he barked out the last word. Turning slowly to face him, I met his angry gaze with my own. "No."

He gave in. "Fine, don't eat now. You will, though. The human body can only go so long without food. Until then, come here!" He rapidly untied my ankles and yanked them until I was no longer propped against the wall. My head hit the floor again, though not as hard as before since I was prepared and had braced myself. Still, I wondered how many more times that could happen without causing permanent damage.

Jeff hovered over me and I feared what he planned to do next. He slid me down until my arms would reach that post again. I attempted to wriggle free, but again, his strength overcame my determination.

I finally gave up and lay still, fearing the worst. But he simply tied my wrists to the post and then sat back in triumph. I knew he thought he'd won—maybe he had. He smiled down at me victoriously. "See, you're already startin' to give up. Maybe after another day you'll finally come to your senses and stay with me so I won't have to keep you tied up."

Quiet tears slid down my cheeks because I imagined he was probably right. I had no fight left in me, just resignation and fear. How many more times would he hit me? How long would he keep me here and what would he do when he was tired of me?

Trembling, I realized he might never let me go. Maybe he planned on holding me hostage forever. Maybe this was his idea of happily ever after.

I must've drifted into a restless sleep once Jeff left, because my mind flitted through several horrific nightmares, The last of which included some very disturbing dialogue between two men.

"How much longer we gonna do this?"

"As long as I feel like it. What's it to you, anyway? You're bein' paid to do a job, so do it!"

"I been doin' it! But I can't keep comin' out here day after day to stand guard while you take your time gettin' the money."

"You gettin' scared on me? If you ain't up for this, I can find somebody who'd be more than happy to make an easy buck."

"Fine, I'll stay. But at least let me get a little action from the tramp."

The sound of a loud *thud* startled me awake, and I realized I hadn't dreamt the voices. They were coming from right outside. "Don't *ever* say that again! She's mine! You touch her and I swear I'll kill you," Jeff roared.

The other voice choked out something unrecognizable, and then the sound of coughing muffled Jeff's swearing. "All right, all right. I was just jokin' around. Won't happen again," I heard the voice say through the coughs.

Gravel crunched closer and closer before the door flew open. I couldn't see outside because of where Jeff had left me, but there was suddenly a rush of air against my exposed stomach. I ached for a shower and clean clothes. I ached for a hot, home-cooked meal. I ached for my warm bed and messy bedroom. Most of all I just ached—physically, mentally, emotionally.

Lying there in fear, waiting for whatever was coming, I thought about how scary Jeff had sounded talking to the guy outside who was apparently paid to ensure I didn't escape. He'd called me "his," and had threatened to kill the guard if he came close to me.

How would I ever get free? And even if I did, where would I go to hide from him? Was he crazy enough to track me down, hunt me? What had happened to him since the time we ended our relationship? He hadn't shown any signs of possessiveness—let alone violence—when we were a couple. At least, I hadn't seen the signs if he did.

The more I thought back on our relationship, the more I questioned the motives behind some of his actions. He had definitely been a jealous boyfriend, but I'd always found that endearing. In fact, I'd been flattered every time he'd threatened a guy whose gaze had lingered just a little too long on me.

With that train of thought, a vision of Landon beaten to a pulp entered my mind before I could stop it. *Oh, no...Oh, Lord, please no!* What if Jeff had done something to him? How would I know? I'd left my cell phone with Kayla, and Landon surely had no idea where to look for me...if he even could. What if Jeff had done something horrible...

I couldn't finish that notion. It was too unbearable. All this time, I'd been thinking about myself—*my* pain and *my* fear. I'd only thought of Landon in the context of him coming to save me, or of him worrying about me.

Selfish. That was the only word that came to mind. Tears began to fall yet again as I contemplated the safety and condition of my sweet, perfect boyfriend. I just couldn't bear the thought of him being tortured. Or worse.

This horrific mental scenario was interrupted by my captor. "Hey, babe, you ready to surrender yet?"

I closed my eyes and begged to pass out. God, please give me peace, I prayed silently. *Just let me faint or something. Please...*

Then—miraculously—everything went dark.

CHAPTER NINETEEN

"There's been serious injury to her head," I heard an unfamiliar voice say. "But she's going to be all right. No permanent brain damage. She may be somewhat delusional when she wakes up, but that's to be expected in this situation. Other than some major bruising and the obvious emotional harm, she'll be fine. It's a miracle, really."

I felt disoriented. There was a strange but steady beeping noise close by, as well as the sound of shuffling footsteps. Several muffled voices told me I was no longer in the abandoned barn—the place that had become my own personal hell.

Hope swelled in my heart and filled my entire being. Had I been rescued? The alien sounds told me I had, but I couldn't see anything. My world was still dark. I panicked for a moment—had I lost my vision?

Then another thought occurred to me…maybe the noises were just a dream. I would wake up and still be in that hellhole. I didn't know which scenario was worse.

"Cora? Can you hear me, sweetheart?" I was definitely dreaming. That sounded like my mother. I tried to force my eyes open, but my eyelids weighed a ton.

"Give her a minute, Betsy. She just regained consciousness. She might not be able to respond yet." And that sounded like my father. Now I was certain it was all a dream. The last thing I remembered was that look of insane hunger in Jeff's eyes...

With that memory, I was fully awake. My eyes flew open, I sat straight up, and curled into a ball, arms hugged to my chest. Wait! Arms to my chest? Nothing was holding my wrists together. I glanced up, observing my surroundings. The white, sterile room was definitely not where I'd been for the last however many days. It was a hospital room.

"Cora!" My mother's face was heaven to me. I was finally safe.

"Mama!" I cried, flinging my arms out as she leaned down to embrace me. Sobs erupted from my chest as I clung to her. I had never felt so overwhelmingly happy in my entire life.

We stayed that way for a few minutes, both of us crying, latched on to one another. I finally noticed my father standing close by, tears rolling down his unkempt face. He looked as if he hadn't shaved in weeks, which was unusual for him.

"Daddy," I whispered. The sight of him crying made my own tears fall even faster. Mama hesitantly released her hold on me and stepped back a few feet, making room for Daddy. I sat up straighter in order to reach my arms around his neck.

"Good to have you back, kid," he muttered in a gruff voice.

When the tears and hugs finally subsided, the questions began. "How'd you find me? Where was I? How long was I there? Where's Jeff? When did—"

"Corabelle," Mama interrupted. "You can relax, honey. Jeffrey Colton has been arrested. But we don't need to talk about this now. We'll answer all your questions when you're better."

The old nickname brought tears to my eyes once again. My parents hadn't called me Corabelle since I was ten years old. I took a deep breath and swallowed the emotions back because I needed to be strong. I needed answers.

"Please...I have to know." When my mom shook her head, I looked at my father. "Daddy, *please*. At least tell me how you found me."

My parents exchanged a glance as if debating whether or not to reveal the sordid details I couldn't remember. Mama sucked in a breath. "You don't remember anything?"

I closed my eyes and shook my head, trying to erase the last memories I had. "The last thing I remember is bein' in that place..." My voice trailed off as I wrestled back more sobs.

"You were unconscious the whole time," my dad remarked. "Makes sense you don't have any recollection of the past twenty-four hours."

"Just twenty-four hours?" I breathed. "Is that how long I was there? It felt like so much longer..."

My mother blinked rapidly and answered with a hoarse voice, "No, sweetie. You've been gone for ten days."

Ten days! I couldn't even fathom it. I'd calculated three days, four at the most. He must have kept me knocked out more than I realized. Or remembered. I suddenly pondered the possibility that he had drugged me. There were times when my memory was a blur, and then I recalled being unable to stay awake for more than what felt like a few hours. However, he hadn't stuck me with any needles, or forced anything down my throat. How would he have gotten the drugs into my system?

Then it hit me. Although I didn't remember eating much, there had always been a fresh glass of water available to me. It was brought in a dark cup, so I couldn't see—and didn't pay much attention to—the contents of that cup. I was so dehydrated that I didn't even take time to smell what I was drinking. And it had tasted enough like tap water...

I considered the existence of a tasteless drug that could knock a person out for hours, or maybe even days, at a time. I certainly wasn't aware of any such evil if it did actually exist, considering the town and home in which I'd been raised.

"Twenty-four hours is just how long it's been since you were found," my dad said, interrupting my disturbing thoughts.

"Oh," I replied. "So how exactly *did* you find me?" I was still determined to learn the details of my escape from hell. My parents looked at each other again, neither of them saying anything. Something was wrong. I swallowed. "Please just tell me...I can handle it."

Daddy cleared his throat and said quietly, "Landon found you."

My heart stopped at the mention of his name. Landon found me. He rescued me. A smile spread across my face, but quickly vanished when I noticed my mother's expression. "What?" I asked. "Why do you look like that? Did somethin' happen to Landon?" I panicked. "Is he okay?"

"There was a struggle, and a gun was pulled," my father began.

My head spun as I tried to comprehend what I'd just been told. A gun was pulled... "Is he...did he...get shot?" I held my breath, waiting painfully for the answer.

Daddy nodded his head. "He did get shot, but it wasn't fatal."

My breath came out in a rush. "So he's okay, then?" There was definitely something else going on. They were acting strange. If the shot wasn't fatal, then why wouldn't they just come right out and say that everything was fine?

Mama spoke next. "Sweetheart, the shot went right into his spinal cord. He's paralyzed from the waist down."

I stiffened. Paralyzed? It couldn't be true. Landon was so strong and vibrant, so full of life…he was invincible. I kicked my legs over the side of the bed. "Where is he? I need to see him."

"Absolutely not! Get back in bed," my father ordered.

"The doctor said you need to stay in bed for at least another day. Your body needs time to rest and heal," Mama chimed in.

"I don't care what the doctor said!" I nearly shouted. "The boy I love is paralyzed because of me. He'll never walk again, or run, or play baseball. His dreams are completely ruined. I have to go to him!"

Mama, being as gentle as she could, pushed me back down on the hospital bed. It didn't take much effort on her part, since the days of food deprivation had left me weak and frail. "You can see him tomorrow. Last we heard, he wasn't even awake yet."

"What do you mean, he wasn't awake?"

"They had to put him to sleep to get the bullet out because of the location."

I closed my eyes and let my head drop against the starch-white pillow. I couldn't believe what was happening. My life—my world—had been perfect a mere twelve days ago. Now everything was messed up. Forever.

Even though I had suffered no external permanent injuries, I felt damaged all the same. I knew I would be haunted for the rest of my life. Something horrific had happened to me, and a person I'd once trusted with my whole heart was responsible. I would never be the same. Then to find out that Landon would never be the same either.

That part was almost harder to deal with than my own tragedy.

CHAPTER TWENTY

The next morning, I awoke to sunlight streaming through the hospital room window. It was the first time I'd seen sunlight in more than ten days. I never even realized how much I'd missed it. Struggling to sit up on the hard bed, I glanced around my temporary home to see if anyone else was present. My gaze landed on the table next to the doorway. It was full of flowers and cards that I hadn't noticed the day before. I felt the tears that I'd become so accustomed to lately, and a small smile spread across my lips. Even though I wasn't aware who each vase of flowers was from, I was touched by the gesture.

Strangely, my parents were nowhere to be found. They'd been there as I'd fallen asleep the previous night, and I'd assumed they would be there still. Horror gripped my chest and I began to panic. What if something had happened to them? A strong sense of loneliness suddenly enveloped me, leaving me breathless and sending me into a full-blown panic attack.

Just then, the door creaked open, and my mother peered in. She rushed to my side the instant she heard me gasping for air. "Cora! What's wrong? Has somethin' happened? Are you hurt?"

For reasons I couldn't even begin to comprehend, sobs escaped my lungs and I shook violently. Taking deep breaths between hysterics, I tried to explain—to my mother and to myself—why I was having a nervous breakdown. "I-I didn't-see anybody....and I thought-you..."

Mama drew me into her arms in an effort to comfort and calm me. "Shh, it's okay. I'm here, sweetie. Mama's here. Nothin's gonna happen now. You're safe."

My breathing slowed as I told myself everything was fine. Only...that was a lie. Everything was *not* fine, I still needed to see Landon.

I shrugged out of my mother's hold and flung my legs off the side of the bed. Bracing myself, I stood too quickly. My legs gave out and I collapsed onto the floor, the room spinning. Mama tried to catch me, but she wasn't quite strong enough. She then pulled me slowly onto the bed, helping me lie back.

I sighed, closing my eyes. "Guess it'll be a while before I'm normal again." *And not just physically.*

Mama stroked my hair. "Just give it time, honey. In a few weeks, you'll feel better and you can put this whole mess behind you."

"Sure, maybe I'll push it to the back of my mind, but it'll never be behind me. Not really. Especially not when Landon's paralyzed. Every time I look at him I'll remember what happened." I peered into my mother's fatigued, worried face and whispered, "How can I ever forget?"

She shook her head, tears filling her sympathetic eyes. "I don't know. Maybe you won't. Maybe instead of forgetting, you'll have to see this tragedy as the thing that makes you stronger, and use it as best you can." We sat in silence for a while, and I pondered what my future held. I lay there, staring at the ceiling, while Mama watched me and held my hand.

Suddenly, I couldn't stand to be in that hospital room, sitting and wallowing in self-pity while Landon dealt with the loss of his life's passion. "I *have* to go see Landon."

"Okay, sweetheart. I'll go find out if he can have visitors. Your daddy should be here soon, and I'll be back quick as I can," Mama said.

As I watched my mother leave, I regretted every mean thing I'd ever said to her in moments of hormonal teen rage. Although our relationship was pretty good overall, there were times I'd let my emotions get the best of me. I'd blamed her for things that weren't at all her fault, and I'd been angry with her for things she'd done to try to make my life better. I realized she only wanted me to be happy. I began to see that she would do everything in her power to keep me safe and healthy. I didn't deserve such a saint looking after me, and I only hoped that someday I would be half the mother she'd always been.

A few minutes later, my dad's voice interrupted my regretful thoughts. "How ya holdin' up today, pumpkin?"

"I'm okay, Daddy," I said unconvincingly.

"Why do I get the feelin' you're lyin' to me?" he asked, leaning in to kiss my forehead.

I inhaled and bit my lip, trying to hold back the tears I could feel swelling in my throat. "I just don't know when I'll be normal again," I whispered. "And I was thinkin' about all the times I've been rude to you and Mama, and now you're both here, takin' care of me and bein' so…unselfish." I paused, shaking my head. "And all I've ever been my whole life is selfish. Even these past couple of days. I'm so consumed with what's happened to me that I've barely even thought about what you and Mama must've been goin' through…or Landon."

Daddy took my hand in his and patted it. "We've all been through a lot, especially your mama. But let me tell you somethin', Cora. You're a good person. Always have been. And by no means are you selfish. This horrible thing happened to *you*. Not to me, not to your Mama, not even to Landon. *You* were the one locked in that God-awful place for ten days. You have every right to be upset, and even selfish, right now. And I'll tell you somethin' else too. The fact that you're worried about bein' selfish just goes to show what a wonderful person you really are."

Those tears I'd been holding back could no longer be contained. "Thank you, Daddy."

"Just tellin' the truth," he answered.

"I don't know what I'd do without you and Mama."

"Well, that's what we're here for, honey. But don't forget to thank the Man upstairs. He's the One who really pulled you from that place."

Leave it to Daddy to bring up religion at a time like this. Sure, I believed in God. And until a couple of weeks ago, I'd always believed He was loving and just. But how could I thank Him for *this*? If He was so loving, how could He let something this horrifying happen to one of His own?

Daddy must have noticed my hesitation, because he decided to elaborate on his statement. "I know that may seem hard to do right now, darlin', but remember, He never lets somethin' happen to us that He won't help us get through. I can't tell you the reason for all this, but there is one. You just gotta have faith."

Just have faith. If only it were that simple.

"Landon's awake," Mama said as she reentered the room. She glanced from my strained expression to Daddy's. "Is everything all right? What's goin' on in here?"

"It's fine, hon," Daddy answered. "We were just talkin' about some tough stuff."

Mama frowned. "Now, George, I hope you're not upsettin' her. All that serious talk can wait, don't you think?"

My father nodded. "Of course." Then he turned his gaze back to me. "Don't you worry about anything so serious right now, pumpkin. You just try to rest and get better."

"I will, Daddy. But first I need to go see Landon."

He shook his head. "You don't need to do that now. You can't even stand. Your Mama told me what happened when you tried to get out of bed."

I'd known he'd try to stop me, but I'd put it off long enough. I had to see Landon. "That's just because I stood up too fast," I said. "I *have* to go to him...now. I've waited long enough."

"But you're—"

"Let her go," Mama interrupted, giving him a look that said he'd better not question her. Then she turned to me. "I'll help you get to his room."

"Okay," I said with relief. "Just let me fix my face. Do you have any makeup with you?"

"Oh, sweetie, I don't think that's such a good idea. Maybe you should wait a little longer before you look in the mirror. I'm afraid you'll just get upset."

She had a point. I hadn't seen myself yet, and I wasn't sure if I could handle what I knew would be repulsive. I could only imagine the bruising. With a heavy heart, I asked, "Then will you do my makeup?"

"Sure," she responded, standing to get her purse. Ten minutes later, she convinced me that I looked "good as new," so we made our way to the elevator and up a couple of floors toward Landon's room. I'd refused the wheelchair Daddy had tried to persuade me to use, so walking was a slow process that involved leaning heavily on Mama and stopping frequently to rest.

When we finally reached our destination and I stood in front of Landon's door, my nerves got the best of me. "I don't know if I can do this," I said quietly. "What if I break down as soon as I see him lyin' in that bed, only able to move half his body?"

"Cora, you love Landon, right?"

"Yeah, I do."

"Then you'll be fine. Even if you cry, I'm sure he'll understand. When you love somebody, you have to learn to get through the tough times together. Otherwise, your relationship will never last. I can see what y'all have is special. It takes most people a lot longer in life to find what you've got with the boy in this room. So go be strong for him, but also know that it's okay to be vulnerable."

"Thanks, Mama." She leaned in to give me a hug and then started back toward the elevator. I stood a minute longer, looking after her. Finally, I inhaled and tried to gain some courage. Landon had risked everything, even his own life, to save me. The least I could do was talk to him. With that thought, I pushed open the door and hoped for strength.

The sight of Landon in that hospital bed was worse than I could have possibly imagined. I wrestled tears the best I could, but the tears won. A sob escaped my lungs as soon as I walked unsteadily through the door.

Landon frowned and reached out his hand. "Hey, Cora, don't cry. It's not as bad as it looks."

I struggled to suck in my sobs then walked the few steps it took to cross the small, sterile room. Standing by his bed, I grasped the hand he offered. "Landon, I'm so sorry this happened to you. How're you feelin'?"

He smiled and kissed the back of my hand. "Much better now that you're here. But what're you doin' outa bed? You gotta be exhausted. Here, sit," he demanded, making room for me next to him. His expression was pained as he struggled to shift his weight with only his arms.

I sat carefully on the edge of the bed, afraid to jostle him too much. "I had to come see you. I've been worried about you."

Chuckling, he asked, "*You've* been worried about *me*?"

I bit my lip, fighting sobs once more. He was putting on a brave front, but I could tell he was terrified. Something in his expression gave it away. "'Course I was worried about you. My parents said you saved my life. What were you thinkin'? You could've been killed!"

Blinking back tears of his own, he answered, "You almost *were* killed. I couldn't let that happen. I'd be nothin' without you, Cora. If you'd died, I might as well have died too."

I clutched his hand more tightly. "Don't say that! You're too special to cast yourself off without a second thought!" He averted his eyes and stared at his hands as the clock ticked. I waited, but he didn't speak. The silence was killing me. "Landon, what's wrong? What're you thinkin' about?"

He squeezed his eyes shut and pounded a fist on the bed. "I'm *not* special...not anymore. The one thing that made me special's ruined now," he muttered, gesturing to his lifeless legs.

Touching his cheek, I turned his face to mine. "You listen to me, Landon. That is *not* the only thing that makes you special. You're more special than anybody I know. You're funny, smart, sweet…and there's somethin' else about you. I can't define it, but it's there. So don't you think for even a *second* that you're less of a person now than you were before. It's not possible."

He looked away again. "But if I can't play baseball—"

"Then you'll find somethin' else to be brilliant at," I insisted.

His eyes met mine and he shook his head. "Listen to me complainin', when you're the one who's been through hell. I should be comfortin' you right now, not the other way around."

Before I could respond, there was a knock on the door and a doctor—Dr. Ketchner, according to his nametag—entered. "How're we doing this morning?" he asked.

"All right, I guess, Doc," Landon replied.

"That's good to hear. I just wanted to let you know we got your test results back, and it looks like we may have overestimated the damage."

"You mean I'm not really paralyzed?"

"Paralysis has most certainly set in, but there's a small chance it might not be permanent like we originally thought."

I squeezed Landon's hand and grinned. "That's great news!"

Oddly, Landon didn't seem to share my excitement. "You said there's a 'small' chance. How small?" he asked.

The doctor's face turned serious as he answered the question. "We're estimating about twenty percent."

"I see."

"I know it may not seem like it, but this is good news. You might walk again. It's a lot to think about, so I'll meet with you and your parents a little later today to discuss your options."

Landon mustered a smile, I assumed to pacify the doctor. "All right. Thanks for lettin' me know."

"You're welcome," Dr. Ketchner said. "I'll leave you alone now. Just buzz me if you need anything." With that, he left and closed the door behind him.

Once we were alone, I turned toward Landon enthusiastically. "You're gonna walk again! That's so great!"

He shook his head. "No, I *might* walk again. But probably not."

I took his face in both my hands and forced him to look into my eyes. "Listen to me. You *will* walk, and you'll play baseball. You'll have a normal life again. Twenty percent's not bad. And you're strong. You're strong, and young, and determined. You *can* do this. It'll take some time and a little hard work, but I believe in you."

A soft smile spread across his lips as he gazed at me in awe. "You're amazing. How can you be so positive after what you've been through?"

I shrugged, and this time, I was the one with averted eyes. "I don't know...I guess...well, maybe if I'm focusin' on you, then I don't have to deal with my own stuff."

"Makes sense, I guess," he said. Then he punched the bed again. "Man, I wish this hadn't happened to you. I should've killed that monster when I had the chance."

My eyes grew wide. "What do you mean, when you had the chance?"

"Guess it's okay to tell you all this now." He inhaled before continuing. "When I didn't hear from you the day you went missin', I called Val. She hadn't talked to you, so I texted Kayla, but she never responded. I waited about an hour, but I had this feelin' somethin' was wrong so I drove to your house. The cops were there, and so were Kayla and Rex."

I stopped him. "Wait, Rex was there?"

Landon cringed. "Yeah, actually if it wasn't for him...well, I don't wanna even think about it. Anyway, your parents were panickin'. I heard your dad tellin' a police officer you'd been taken from the mall. The first thought that went through my mind was that Jeff took you, so I told everybody about the secret admirer notes and the bruise he left on your arm." Landon paused.

"What is it?" I asked. "What happened?"

"Apparently, Jeff had been plannin' this for a while. Rex said he noticed some guy creepin' around your house a couple months ago. He didn't know at the time it was Jeff, but when he described the guy and his truck, we knew."

My breath came out in a rush. Jeff was even more demented than I'd thought.

"You okay?" Landon asked.

"I...yeah..."

"We can stop. You don't have to know all the details right now."

"No, go ahead. I need to know."

Landon hesitated. "If you're sure..."

I nodded, and he continued. "Well, Rex thought it was strange this kid was hangin' around your house without anybody home, so he waited for Jeff to leave and then got in his car and followed him. He said Jeff turned down an old dirt road, but it was all washed out from the rain we'd been gettin', and he couldn't make it through in his car. That's when your mom mentioned that Jeff's parents used to own a barn where they kept their horses. She didn't know exactly where it was, but Rex gave the cops a pretty good start. So—"

"You went there yourself, didn't you?" I interrupted.

His eyes closed for a moment. When they opened again, I saw the emotions he must've felt at that moment. With a pained expression, he continued. "I couldn't just sit back and do nothin', so I went lookin' for the barn. But I couldn't find it, and neither could

[175]

the cops. I swear to you, I searched for you every day." He paused, a look of guilt shrouding his expression.

"Landon, it's not your fault. None of this is your fault."

Landon looked at the ground and continued his story, ignoring my remark. "Jeff's parents wouldn't cooperate with police. They refused to give 'em the address of that barn. Said they'd sold it a long time ago to a construction company that tore it down. But they were lyin'. They were just tryin' to protect him. Didn't even care what he was doin' to you."

Landon's mouth pursed into an angry line for a moment. When he began to speak again, his tone was distant, as if he'd gone back in time. "They finally caved when the cops took 'em in for questioning. Don't know why it took so long for that to happen. We could've found you a lot sooner... Anyway, I got there first, and I saw Jeff hit you. Then I noticed his gun on the ground next to him, and I thought about grabbin' it and shootin' him. But that wasn't good enough. I couldn't stand the sight of him doin' that to you. I got mad. So mad...I rushed him and forgot about the gun. I just wanted to beat the life out of him. And that's what I tried to do after I pulled him off you. We wrestled back and forth a few minutes, and I didn't know he'd grabbed his gun. When I finally heard the police sirens, I pushed him back and started runnin' toward the door to wave 'em down. That's when he pulled the trigger. Lucky for me, the cops busted in before he could get in another shot."

I shuddered and threw my arms around him. "Landon...I'm so glad you're okay!" I exclaimed, hugging him as tightly as possible. My tears soaked his shirt as we embraced. "Don't ever let me go," I whispered.

"Not in a million years." We clung to each other, both aware that what had happened could have ended in another way—a much worse way.

CHAPTER TWENTY-ONE

Two weeks later, alone in my bedroom and gazing at the serene outdoors from my cushioned window seat, I couldn't escape the terrifying images that clouded my memory. Sleep had not come easily since I'd awakened from my real-life nightmare to a stale hospital room. Peace had become a sensation I could hardly remember, because each time I closed my eyes, I saw Jeff. He was there on top of me, tying my wrists to that awful post and hitting my face, stealing the blissful ignorance I'd once had regarding evil in this world.

A knock on the door startled me back to the present. I turned my gaze away from the clear blue sky and toward the doorway as Val and Kayla entered. It was the first time I'd seen them since being taken captive. I'd refused visitors while in the hospital, promising to have the girls over as soon as I was settled at home.

"Is there room on that seat for two more?" Val asked.

"Hey!" I exclaimed, standing to greet them. First Valerie, then Kayla, hugged me.

Kayla lingered a bit longer than Val, leaning back to look in my face. "I'm so sorry, Cora. I feel like what happened to you was my fault. I'll never forgive myself."

"Kay, don't say that!" I responded. "It was *not* your fault! At all!"

"No, it was. If I hadn't let you walk to that trashcan alone, or if I'd just been payin' attention…"

I shook my head. "There's no way you could've known somethin' like this would happen. I mean, it was still daylight, for Pete's sake! *Please* don't blame yourself, because I don't blame you in any way. Jeff had the whole thing planned out. If I hadn't been at the mall that day, he would've found me another time…" I trailed off, recalling how I'd once loved, hugged, and willingly kissed my attacker. I'd shared my secrets, fears, hopes, and dreams with him. He'd been an intimate part of my life. I shuddered.

"Are you okay?" Val asked with concern. "You look pale."

"Yeah, maybe you should sit down," Kayla added.

"Okay," I mumbled, walking slowly toward my bed. I sank down, zombie-like. "I let him into my heart. I let a violent psycho into my heart. I was so close to him…" I closed my eyes and attempted to erase all the visions—both good and bad—of him.

My friends sat with me while I rehashed the events of my trauma with them. I told them everything I remembered, from when I was taken from the parking lot to when I woke up in the hospital. I could see the looks of horror on their faces, but once I'd started talking, I couldn't stop. Everything came pouring out. They tried their best to comfort me and it felt good to know they cared. When a couple of hours had passed, we all sat silent, exhausted. There was nothing more to say.

We jumped when Kayla's phone rang. Her mom wanted her to go home.

As soon as they'd each given me one more hug and left the room, Mama appeared at my door. "Knock, knock," she said. "How's it goin' in here?"

"I'm okay, Mama."

"Listen, sweetie. I've been thinkin'. Since you missed your graduation ceremony and your birthday's comin' up, why don't we have a party for you? Would you like that?"

A party? I'd been locked up and held captive for ten days and I'd missed one of the biggest milestones of my life. That didn't exactly scream "Let's celebrate!" Besides, I'd completely forgotten about my birthday until that very moment.

"I don't know…" I trailed off, hesitating long enough for her to get the hint. "Not sure I'm up for it."

She nodded and pursed her lips. "It's your decision. I just thought it might take your mind off things for a while. Keep you occupied. But I don't wanna make you uncomfortable…just promise me you'll think about it."

"All right, Mama. I'll think about it," I replied, even though I already knew my answer. My stomach turned to knots at just the *thought* of socializing and pretending to be okay. I couldn't handle a party. All I wanted for my birthday was to go back in time and erase those ten days. Unfortunately, time travel was not possible.

After that conversation with my mother, I assumed the party subject was dropped—at least for a while—but before I went to bed that evening, my father brought it up again. "Your mama said you don't want a birthday party this year," he commented when he came to tell me goodnight.

I groaned internally but tried not to let my frustration show. I knew my parents only wanted to make me happy. "I just don't know if it's the right time," I explained. "I don't really have a reason to celebrate."

My father frowned. "I know it seems that way, darlin', but you've got plenty to celebrate. Like the fact that you're alive and home, and that Landon's alive. That shot could've been fatal." With a sympathetic smile, he continued. "You can also celebrate that the police got Jeff and that he's locked up for a long time. He won't ever be able to hurt you again."

Everything he said made sense, but I couldn't bring myself to agree to the party whole-heartedly. So I said, "I know you're right, Daddy. But I just can't do it..."

"Cora, remember that talk we had when you were in the hospital?" He paused, taking my hand in his. "I told you you're not at all selfish, because what you've been through happened to you and not anybody else?"

"Yeah..." I replied hesitantly. "So it should be my decision whether or not to have this party, right?"

"You're right, it's absolutely your decision. But I think your family and friends would appreciate a chance to celebrate with you. It's not at all selfish for you to think about what you've been through and what you're still goin' through, but it might be selfish to push away the people who love you."

"What?" Blinking back the tears that suddenly pooled behind my eyelids, I jerked my hand out of his grip. "Just because I don't want a party doesn't mean I'm pushin' people away," I replied defensively.

He pursed his lips. "Listen, I know you've been through hell...a far worse hell than I could ever imagine. But I want you to think about your mama. She's been through it, too. We thought we'd lost you, and that ripped her to pieces. Then to find out you were alive, and what happened to you...it was like puttin' her back together then rippin' her apart all over again." He sighed. "You can't understand this now, but one day when you have kids, you will.

She feels everything you feel. Knowin' what that kid did to you hurts her more than you realize. She needs to have this party to celebrate gettin' you back."

I blinked. He was right, I'd been selfish. I hadn't even considered what my parents had gone through while I was missing. It couldn't have been easy, to say the least. What kind of daughter would I be if I couldn't fake a few smiles and eat some cake?

I nodded. "Okay, tell her to go ahead with the plans. But don't tell her we had this talk. I don't wanna upset her. Just tell her...tell her I had a change of heart."

Daddy smiled and kissed my forehead. "Sure. Now sleep tight, Corabelle."

Mama arranged the party for the weekend after my birthday, leaving us just shy of three weeks to plan everything. She went all out, renting a tent, tables, chairs, and a wooden dance floor. She chose a spot in the corner of the backyard as the celebration destination. Strings of white lights dangled around the tent, and crystal vases holding pink roses served as centerpieces for the fuchsia cloth-covered tables. Also scattered across the tables were small diamond-shaped glass beads. A light pink aisle runner led the way from our pool deck to the tent. For added romance, miniature lanterns lined both sides of the runner.

Because she wanted the evening to be elegant, Mama sent out formal invitations that included the phrase "cocktail attire." This was shaping up to be *the* event of the year, and my parents had even hired a DJ. I had no idea how she'd managed to plan such a huge affair in such a short amount of time, but she had. Leave it to my mama to conquer the impossible.

On the morning of the big day, I actually awoke feeling excited. All the plotting and decorating had worked its effect on me. We'd invited thirty guests, and they were due to arrive at eight o'clock that evening.

After I'd jumped eagerly out of bed, I gently ran my fingers across the new dress Mama had insisted I get for the big occasion. "You only turn eighteen once," she'd remarked.

It was a beautiful pink satin party dress that fell a couple of inches above my knees. The strapless masterpiece was fitted at the bust and waist and slightly puffed out at the bottom. The sweetheart neckline was adorned with brilliant rhinestones which complemented the rhinestones on the silver strappy heels that were a birthday surprise from my parents. To complete the look, I decided to hot-roll my hair and borrow my mother's one-carat diamond stud earrings.

But there was still plenty to do before I could play dress-up, so I skipped downstairs to find Mama mixing together the ingredients for what I assumed would be my birthday cake. "What can I do to help?" I asked.

She looked up from her batter. "Oh, mornin', sweetie." She paused. "Hmm, well the tent's all ready, so I guess the only thing we have to do today is the food. Here, you can chop these up for the salad."

"Okay," I replied, grabbing the electric chopper from a cabinet under the counter. I threw in a cucumber first and hit the start button. While the chopper worked, I watched Mama pour the cake batter into a pan. "Thanks for doin' all this," I said. "I know I wasn't on board with the whole idea at first, but everything's turned out so great, and I'm really excited."

She met my gaze and smiled. "You're welcome. It's been fun. You know how I like to entertain. I'm just glad you're happy."

We chopped, stirred, baked, and cooked in contented silence for the next couple of hours. The final results of our labor included a salad, pineapple sandwiches cut into circles, a vegetable platter, a colorful bowl of fruit, croissants filled with turkey and cheese, the birthday cake, and various other delicious treats my mother created that I didn't even know what to call.

"That should do it. Let's stick all this in the fridge," Mama instructed. "We'll wait 'til about seven fifteen to put it out."

I did as I was told and asked if there was anything else that needed to be finished before the guests arrived. After my mother assured me that there was nothing else she needed help with at the moment, I decided it was safe to begin my beauty regimen.

I headed upstairs to start getting ready for the party. After a long, relaxing shower and over an hour of fussing with hair and makeup, it was finally time to put on the dress.

The satin material felt wonderful against my skin, hugging my curves in just the right places. A look in the full-length mirror hanging on my bedroom door confirmed how well the shape worked with my figure. I'd worried this particular dress would be too frivolous, but the reflection I saw radiated nothing but elegance. I hadn't felt this beautiful in a long time.

Ever since I'd been kidnapped, I'd felt unattractive, though I wasn't quite sure why. I hadn't felt in the least bit beautiful, or elegant, or even pretty. But on this day, staring at the person in front of me, I could see a future for myself again, which included all the possibilities that Jeff had tried to steal from me.

My mother's voice snapped me out of my trance. "It's time to set out the food," she called.

"Comin'!" I walked barefoot out of my room and down the stairs, careful not to let my dress catch on anything.

Mama gasped as she saw me enter the kitchen. "You look absolutely stunning!" she exclaimed with tears in her eyes.

"Now, Mama, none of that." I smiled as she started to get choked up. "Tonight's a celebration!"

She wiped her eyes. "I know it is, sweetie. It's a celebration of your life—the day you were born and the day we got you back."

I had to turn away from her and take a deep breath to prevent my own tears. I was so touched—I could never have asked for a better mother. "Thanks, Mama," I managed to reply through a tight throat. "Okay, let's get this stuff out before people start showin' up."

We walked through the kitchen onto the deck, then down the deck steps to the path Mama had created. We made it to the tent and arranged the food on the specified tables. I paused to observe my surroundings once we were finished. The dance floor occupied the center of the tent, the food tables were in one corner, the DJ's table was across the dance floor from the food, and the rest of the tables were scattered throughout the tent. The final outcome was incredible—even prom couldn't compare to how great everything looked.

As we made our way back to the house, I praised and thanked Mama again. "You did such an awesome job!" I exclaimed, adding, "It's even better than prom! Thank you so much. I really appreciate everything you did."

She smiled. "I'd do it all again in a heartbeat."

A few minutes later, I was back in my room, checking to make sure hair and makeup were still in place. I'd just sat down on the edge of my bed when I heard the doorbell ring. Excitement washed over me as I jumped up to grab the box my new shoes were in. I opened the box and took the shoes out, pausing for a minute to admire them, and then slipped my feet in and buckled the straps. I stood again, took one last glance in the mirror, and headed for the stairs. Before I could make it even halfway down, Val and Kayla ambushed me, and both began chattering at once.

"You look so good!"

"Oh, my goodness, you're beautiful!"

"Is anybody else here yet?"

"I wanna go see how the tent looks!"

I couldn't decipher who was saying what, but their enthusiasm made me grin. "Slow down, y'all." I laughed. "I can't hear anything when y'all are talkin' at the same time!"

Val grinned. "Sorry, we're just excited!"

"Okay, well, I'm ready, so we can go outside. Mama put Daddy in charge of greetin' everybody and showin' them to the tent, but since y'all are the first ones here, follow me!"

The girls gushed about how beautiful everything looked for a good five minutes once we got to the festive tent. The DJ was already playing music and the lighting was all set. They couldn't get over how my mother had pulled it all off in just three weeks.

"Don't ask me," I remarked. "She's Superwoman, I guess! I just hope people show up since we didn't give much notice."

"I don't think you have to worry about that," Kayla replied. "Everybody in town's been talkin' about this. Even the ladies at the salon where my mom gets her hair done know about it."

Val squeezed my hand with anticipation. "It's *the* event of the year!"

Butterflies fluttered around in my stomach as we waited on more people to arrive. By five minutes 'til eight, I was pacing. Just as my two best friends were assuring me that people would show up any minute, a group of eight of our classmates entered the tent, followed shortly after by another large group, and then by a few couples. In less than an hour, the tent was filled to capacity.

I made my way around the party, greeting friends and feeling completely overwhelmed with gratitude for all the people who cared enough to share this night with me. But as the DJ got the party warmed up and people began to hit the dance floor, my mind was elsewhere. I joined the dancing for a couple of songs, but I couldn't completely relax because Landon still hadn't arrived.

It was unlike him to show up anywhere late, especially when I was involved. I'd visited him in the hospital every day until he was released, and then I'd kept him company at home. The last time we'd seen each other was two days ago, with the understanding that I'd be too busy to leave the house until after the party.

When Landon still hadn't arrived an hour later, I began to worry. Fighting panic, I consulted Valerie and Kayla. "This isn't like him," I whispered. "He's always early, and I figured tonight he'd wanna be by my side as people got here." Closing my eyes, I let out a shaky breath and wondered aloud, "What if somethin' happened?"

Kayla put an arm around my shoulders and tried to put my fears to rest. "Nothin' happened," she said. "I'm sure he's just runnin' late."

"Yeah," Val chimed in. "Maybe it takes him longer now, ya know?"

Of course. Why hadn't I thought of that? I'd been so wrapped up in my party that his handicap had completely slipped my mind. Until that very moment, I'd been expecting him to come walking through the door. My throat constricted with sudden unshed tears as I realized that wouldn't be the case.

"You're probably right," I mumbled. "Guess I didn't think about that." With a heavy heart, I turned my head toward the tent entrance, wishing more than anything that I *could* see him walk through it.

The DJ's voice suddenly boomed over the speakers, interrupting my secret moment of grief. "Listen up, all you party animals! It's time to wish our birthday girl a happy eighteenth!" he announced. "And we've got a special surprise just for that! Come on in here, kid!"

Landon wheeled his chair through an opening in the back of the tent, just behind the DJ's table. I glanced at Valerie and Kayla to see if I could detect any sort of sly expression on their faces that would imply they knew something about this "surprise," but they seemed as confused as I felt.

Taking the microphone from the DJ, Landon locked eyes with me and began to speak. "Cora Stephens, you're the best thing that ever happened to me," he said. "I've never met anybody so thoughtful, smart, funny, or just plain awesome. You're beautiful—inside *and* out. I don't know what I would've done without you these past few weeks. You've been there for me, even when I wasn't easy to deal with." He paused and inhaled, then smiled. "Now, get your pretty self up here so I can give you your birthday present."

My heart pounded as I glided toward him. I felt so overwhelmed that I had to remind myself to put one foot in front of the other.

Taking my hand as soon as it was in reach, Landon continued. "I know things haven't turned out like you always thought they would this year. A horrible thing happened to you, but you still laugh. You still encourage everybody around you to be a better person, just like you always have. You're the strongest girl I know. I think you deserve so much more than this," he said, handing me a jewelry box, "but it's all I could afford."

I glanced at the box as it entered my grasp, then back at him. "Landon, you didn't have to do this," I whispered.

He smiled that wonderful smile I loved so much and whispered back, "I wanted to."

My hands trembled as I opened the box. A heart-shaped diamond pendant looped through a delicate silver chain shone up at me. I gasped. "It's beautiful!"

He spoke into the microphone again. "I want you to know you've got my heart. Hopefully you'll remember that every time you wear this one." He put the microphone down and took the necklace out of its box, motioning for me to lean down. I ducked my head toward him, and he gently placed the necklace around my neck and fastened the clasp.

Teary eyed, I whispered a soft "Thank you," and kissed his cheek.

"You're welcome, but that's only the first part of your birthday present."

I frowned—hoping he hadn't spent more money on me—and watched as he rolled his chair through the crowd and onto the center of the dance floor. He gripped both handles of his wheelchair, grinning from ear to ear. Then, he planted his feet firmly on the ground and slowly began to lift his upper body. My eyes widened as the realization of what he was attempting to do struck me. I wanted to scream at him to stop, that he would hurt himself! But I couldn't. I stood frozen in place, holding my breath. There was complete silence throughout the tent as everyone watched Landon in anticipation.

With one final determined effort, he pushed himself out of the chair and stood, facing me confidently. With a huge smile, he asked, "Can I have this dance?"

At that moment, I regained control of my body and ran to him. Seeing that I was headed straight for him and not slowing down, Landon put his hands out, cautioning me to be careful. I came to an abrupt stop before him and took the hand he offered. He then wrapped both his arms around my waist, and my fingers linked together around his neck. A slow, romantic tune began to play and we held each other, swaying slowly back and forth.

"I'm recoverin' a lot faster than the doctors expected," he murmured. "I was determined to dance with you on your birthday, even before you planned this party." The tears I'd been holding in could no longer be contained and began to make their way down my cheeks.

"Oh, Landon!" I breathed. "For you to walk again…that's all I want for my birthday. Or ever." He pulled me tighter, and our bodies continued to move in perfect harmony—with each other and with the music.

And at that precious moment, I knew we'd both be all right. I knew that whatever plans I'd had before mine and Landon's misfortune happened no longer mattered. I suddenly saw my life in a completely new light. The only thing that mattered anymore was being here with Landon, helping him through his recovery, and working out my own issues.

I realized that, despite all attempts to convince myself otherwise, I was actually *not* okay. I would be, but it would take time. I began to understand that in order to make myself truly happy again, I needed to "just have faith," which is exactly what my father had said that day in the hospital.

I gazed at Landon through my lashes and reached up to plant a gentle kiss on his lips, simultaneously saying a silent prayer of gratitude.

Thank You, God, for sending Landon to save me from that awful place. Thank You for giving me such amazing family and friends who support and love me, even when I don't deserve it. Most of all, thank You for this beautiful tragedy I call my life.

ABOUT THE AUTHOR

Born and raised in a small Georgia town, Emily Paige Skeen takes from her own life experiences to create real, relatable characters for her novels. She loves to intertwine small-town charm with deep emotion and intrigue, creating stories that inspire readers.

When she's not writing or chasing after her two youngsters—both under the age of five—you can find Emily reading, soaking up the sun whenever possible, or shopping. She, her husband, and their kids make their home in a tiny little town an hour south of Atlanta, on a five-acre plot of land right off a bumpy red-dirt road. She loves to sit and listen as the ever-present crickets and frogs perform their harmonious concerts in the still, quiet evening hours.

Writing has always been Emily's passion, ever since she crafted her first sloppily hand-written story plastered over spiral notebook paper at the emotionally-charged age of thirteen. Now, she strives to encourage and inspire girls and young women with her writing. She believes that with a little bit of faith and a whole lot of love, anything's possible.

Thank you for your Prism Book Group purchase! Visit our website to enjoy free reads, great deals, and entertaining, wholesome fiction!

http://www.prismbookgroup.com

Are you struggling with your own tragedy? God is ready and waiting to see you through with His perfect love.

"Do not be anxious about anything, but in every situation, by prayer and petition, with thanksgiving, present your requests to God. And the peace of God, which transcends all understanding, will guard your hearts and your minds in Christ Jesus." Philippians 4:6-7